The Magic Door

Awesome Adventures

Edited By Briony Kearney

First published in Great Britain in 2023 by:

Young Writers
Remus House
Coltsfoot Drive
Peterborough
PE2 9BF
Telephone: 01733 890066
Website: www.youngwriters.co.uk

Printed and bound in the UK by BookPrintingUK
Website: www.bookprintinguk.com
YB0540U

Foreword

Welcome reader, come on in and enter a world of imagination!

This book is jam-packed full of stories on a whole host of topics. The Magic Door was designed as an introduction to creative writing and to promote an enjoyment of reading and writing from an early age.

A simple, fun activity of imagining a door and what might lie on the other side gave even the youngest and most reluctant writers the chance to become interested in literacy, giving them the key to unlock their creativity! Pupils could write a descriptive piece about what lay beyond their door or a complete adventure, allowing older children to let their ideas flow as much as they liked, encouraging the use of imagination and descriptive language.

We live and breathe creativity here at Young Writers – it gives us life! We want to pass our love of the written word onto the next generation and what better way to do that than to celebrate their writing by publishing it in a book!

Each awesome author in this book should be super proud of themselves, and now they've got proof of their imagination and their ideas when they first started creative writing to look back on in years to come!

There is nothing like the imagination of children, and this is reflected in the adventures in this anthology. I hope you'll enjoy reading their first stories as much as we have.

Contents

Jacob Rendall (10)	64
Honey Prowse (10)	65
Harry Thomson (10)	66
Zethar Savage (10)	67
Aimee Maddern (10)	68
Mylee Reynolds (11)	69
Cherry-Mae O'keife (9)	70
Mason Ziwange (9)	71
Willow Trevail (8)	72
Zachary Timings (10)	73
Libby Cringle (9)	74
Daisy Coates (8)	75
Isla-Grace Walker (9)	76
Emilie Marshall (9)	77
Ethan Billinger (9)	78
Riley Buckingham (10)	79
Morgan Buckingham (10)	80
Ruby Spencer (9)	81
Amelie Furse (9)	82
Ziva Lang (8)	83
Lily Bawden-Bonell (8)	84
Jasmine Wright (9)	85
Niayah Wildman (8)	86
Sophia Tonkin (9)	87
Logan Anderson (9)	88
Lizzie Strick (9)	89

St Mary's Catholic Primary School, Broadway

Darcey Mottram (10)	90
Noah Skidmore (9)	92
Anna Sijo (10)	94
Oscar Ford (11)	96
Beau Bromley (9)	98
William Hobbs-Gray (9)	100
Emma Terefenko (9)	102
Harry Dempsey (9)	104
Maddie Emms (10)	106
Harry Tarte (9)	107
Taylor Miller (9)	108

St Mary's Catholic Primary School, Evesham

Lilly Arens (10)	109
Weronika Grosfeld (8)	110
Samanta Witalec (9)	112
Oliwia Kustra (9)	114
Sophia Dare (8)	116
Jessica Whiting (10)	118
Dexter Wright (9)	120
Jakub Kupejtys (9)	122
Ruairidh Marlborough (8)	124
Jack Kingsbury (9)	126
Jacob Hughes (8)	127
Eva Fairburn-Shead (7)	128
William Kizas (9)	129
Weronika Jaskulska	130
Riya Elsa Joby (10)	131
Luca Kear-Bertie (9)	132
Joshua Hosken (10)	133
Logan Hart (9)	134
Zach Thompson (8)	135
Dominik Gyorgy (8)	136
Frank Johnson (10)	137
Harry Simpson (8)	138
Ella-Rose Bools (7)	139
Rebecca Adenuga (10)	140
Henry Resende (9)	141
Nothando Ganse (10)	142
Orlagh Turner (10)	143
David Rusnak (11)	144
Anastazia Kalinska (7)	145
Michal Skowronski (10)	146
Joanna Watalska (8)	147
Kipras Price (8)	148
Felix Hudson (5)	149
Albert Duta (10)	150
Olivia Kilian (10)	151
Jack Ciesar (6)	152
Olivia Nind (8)	153
Leon Philip (8)	154
Blanka Indyk (5)	155
Rohan Wright (5)	156
Erin Fitzpatrick (5)	157

Cristian La Barbera (5)	158
Ava Withers (5)	159
Esther Olabamiji (6)	160
Anthoina Podsada (5)	161
Foster Marlborough (5)	162
Theo Lancaster (5)	163
Udyat Udyat (7)	164
Aeiden Reigon (5)	165

Trinity Oaks CE Primary School, Horley

Cara (7)	166
Lincoln Pulham (7)	168
Harrison Thompson-Gay (7)	169
Thando Samira Muringai (6)	170
Georgina Varghese (6)	171
Freya Wicks (6)	172
Digby (7)	173
Edward Meech (6)	174
Rafael Sweeney (6)	175
Drew Bastin-Curd (7)	176
Max O'Driscoll (7)	177

The Stories

The Vampire Dimension

One day, a girl named Rose was doing her make-up when she felt the Earth shaking. She got so worried that she hid under the bed. It stopped shaking but there was a beam of light coming from the door. What was behind the door?

She got out from under the bed then tiptoed to the door, hearing thunder. She opened the door so fast, she felt the air whooshing through. The wind pushed her in and she was dragged to a different world. The wind stopped and she was dropping from the sky. She fainted and nearly bashed her head, but a handsome man caught her.

She woke up in the hospital with the man who saved her. She asked, "Who are you?"

The boy said, "I am a vampire, but I barely drink blood."

She said okay and told him how she got there. He said his door was flashing and he took her there. A vampire was chasing them but they made it to the door. She opened the door and said goodbye. She promised herself that she would never go back there again.

Taiyon Jones (11)
Allen Edwards Primary School, Stockwell

Millie In Wonderland

I opened my eyes. Where was I? What happened to me? The last thing I remembered was opening the little purple door that appeared in my bedroom. Slowly, I got up and looked around. I couldn't believe it. I was sure I recognised this magical land with the peculiar plants and animals, but where from? Then it hit me: Alice in Wonderland!

As I ran through the lush grass, the warm wind blowing through my hair, I caught sight of the fairies and little elf-like creatures. I could hear the distant sound of laughter and a faint spray of rushing water. I descended deeper into this fantasy world when something caught my eye.

There I saw it - the long wooden table that was underneath a huge oak tree, filled with cakes and pies and warm drinks. And there, seated at either end, were the Mad Hatter and the March Hare, having tea. It was just like the book! I stood in awe of this incredible scene and slowly walked toward it in disbelief.

Suddenly, the Mad Hatter approached me and asked me to have a seat. With just a moment's hesitation, I accepted and helped myself to a little round cake. It was sweet and tasted faintly of strawberries. He told me many stories of growing up in Wonderland. A few hours later, it felt like we were life-long friends. I never wanted to leave, but I knew it was time to go home.

Olivia Frisby (10)
Allen Edwards Primary School, Stockwell

The Magic Door

There was a mysterious, spine-tingling door that stood high and proud in the daylight like a mesmerising champion. As I ambled toward the bizarre door, sweat trickled down my forehead. But the way this frightening door was tempting me, this chance could not be lost.

After a long think about whether I would regret my decision, I heaved the door. Around me was a different world. Straight after, the peculiar door vanished. Out of the corner of my eye, I saw buildings burning down, causing them to collapse to the floor. There was fire. It spread as quickly as a cheetah and sprinted to each house.

There were people dashing out of their nearly demolished houses, trying to save their lives. Wood and straw hit the dusty, rocky houses and bashed the floor. Against my feet, wood and straw brushed with every step. Others who were trying to escape the colossal danger barged their way through.

People were screaming at the top of their lungs. There was fire all around. I sprinted, looking for the door that caused all this chaos. I found it and dashed in to escape. Finally, I was safe.

Edward Mersah (9)
Allen Edwards Primary School, Stockwell

The Magic Door

Standing before me was a giant and heavy door. I began to push with all my might and before I knew it, I was trapped in an enclosed room. Then I realised I wasn't alone. On the other side of the room was an angry, hungry, and threatening creature.

I ran toward the wall, then looked. I realised it moved toward me. I quickly realised it was playing with me. I couldn't take my eyes off it. There was nothing I could do, I took a glance to my left then looked back. That was enough time to corner me. The creature had thick and bubbly skin. I stepped back and hit a button. Suddenly, a secret passage opened, revealing the door. I ran toward it, then it closed off. It was a trap. The creature began to crawl toward me. Its bones cracked, its eyes widened, it got ready to attack...

I noticed an axe beside me. I used all my strength to pick it up.

Jacob Cassidy (11)
Allen Edwards Primary School, Stockwell

The Old Curiosity Shop

I opened the door and saw an antique shop. My eyes gazed as they saw thousands upon thousands of trinkets and clothes.

Nearly all of the shop was wooden. There was an oak bookshelf filled to the brim with curiosities from all over the universe. There even was a wooden kettle. The only non-wooden trinket was a black steel pocket watch. It was cold and heavy in my hands.

In the corner of my eye, I saw a scripture that said: 'what is old was new and what is new will become old'. An old man was sitting at the front desk. He was hunched over as if he was sleeping. He looked quite smart, as did the shop. On his wrist lay a tin watch that looked extremely broken and scruffy, in contrast to the shop.

A cuckoo clock ticked amongst the silence and the smell of polish tickled my nose. The shop was enveloped with an atmospheric feeling.

Faiz Agoro (10)

Allen Edwards Primary School, Stockwell

The Tropical Island

I stepped into the magic door. Suddenly, I came flying from the sky, landing on a hard but soft surface. Without a warning, I woke up to the sound of a beautiful tropical paradise.

It was incredible! In every corner of my eye, I could see animals playing around, such as monkeys, parrots, and even snakes. I could also hear birds chirping, trees waving side to side, and much more. This was the best thing ever.

Immediately, I saw something in the distance and started to follow it. After a while of travelling, I spotted a peculiar figure. Eventually, it started to move toward me. Before it could attack, I ran straight out of there.

Just then, a massive volcano started to erupt, spitting out lava, destroying everything in its way. Before anything could touch me, I ran as fast as I could back into the magic door.

Kian Corrales Luzi (10)
Allen Edwards Primary School, Stockwell

The Magic Door

The ancient, broken door appeared all of a sudden, covered with graves and monsters, inviting me to the unknown. The door had mysteries lurking inside. The mist hissed from the door.

After I stepped inside, I saw skeletons laughing and jumping like bouncy balls. As well as this, the hazy, strong wind blew the glass out of the windows and shattered it across the mud, sinking into it. The strange coffin opened wide and a flesh-eating vampire appeared.

The ripped, cracked ceiling hung like a spiderweb. The murky, disgusting pond burst out polluted air. The crooked door banged behind me. As I looked out, the lopsided graves stared at me. In the distance, dusty, creaking stairs coughed and sneezed. My heart beat so rapidly. The gross spiderwebs tangled around the house, stuffed with flies.

Yara Araho (10)
Allen Edwards Primary School, Stockwell

The Unusual Magic Door

The gloomy, dark door stood in the middle of the hall. The door handle glimmered in the dark. As I walked closer, I saw bloodstained handprints. After hauling and yanking, it creaked and in the centre, there was an unfamiliar, bizarre house. I walked in anyway. I heard a loud, ear-splitting scream. My soul jumped out of my skin! When I looked down, I saw human bones!

As I opened the door, lights danced and flickered. The wall cracked and bats flew out of the house in fear. The grey, dusty stairs creaked as I stepped on them. Everything in the house was weird and old. Then a hand tapped my shoulder.

As I looked behind me, a person waved to me. But for some reason, I couldn't feel her. I was confused. When I finally came to my senses, I realised I was talking to a ghost!

Annabelle Boateng (9)

Allen Edwards Primary School, Stockwell

Dungeon

I opened a magic door that had tentacles surrounding it, trying to keep it shut. I walked through. Suddenly, I was falling out of the sky. I eventually landed on a mysterious substance in a dungeon.

I looked everywhere to find out there were chains hanging from the ceiling. There was blood dripping down the walls. I felt scared, wanting to run back through the door, just to find out the door had vanished.

Heat pounded me. Sweat was already falling off my face. Red pillars had formed, circling a dragon. A sword and shield fell into my hands. The dragon had fire-breathing attacks. I used my shield to parry, but my shield was only wood so it set on fire easily.

I was able to get a quick hit and found out that with every hit, a shard of the door opened.

Dylan Martins (10)
Allen Edwards Primary School, Stockwell

The Weird Beach

The magic door appeared in front of me, standing there like a statue. As I opened the door, I realised the other half of the door was covered in sand. As I went inside, I was shocked to see a beach. Not just a regular beach, but a beach with un-living things, like the water and sand, alive and talking!
It was beautiful. The beach was moon-glow gold. The sea looked dozy as it rested in the afternoon glow. I was walking on a horseshoe of beach. Towers of radiant light soaked the sea with their beauty. The mix of colours, the mix of shapes, the mix of sizes, it was a thrill.
All the sea animals played in the sea, splashing the water as a result. The rocks stood as still as statues. I instantly knew that I was in paradise.

Rodrigo Costa (9)
Allen Edwards Primary School, Stockwell

The Magic Door

I woke up at my house as usual and saw a white shining light coming out of my cupboard. I went up to it and opened the door. To my surprise, I saw a white and glistening door that was just there, floating in my cupboard.

When I opened the heavy metal door, I stepped in and, suddenly, I was in WWII and some people were harassing me because they thought I was from Poland. They were throwing stuff at me. I ran for my life and caught my breath. The bricks were falling all along and the smoke was making me tired.

I tried my best to continue running and, thankfully, to the next left I saw the magic door. I saw houses being broken apart and people holding their parents' hands, shaking, and smoke fading away into the sky.

Yusra Sheikh (10)
Allen Edwards Primary School, Stockwell

The Wonders Of Space

I went through the door and witnessed a blue Earth with stars surrounding it like a cover, tighter and tighter. As I was floating around, stars were shining gloriously in the vacuum of space.

I could hear my breathing in my helmet. My heart was beating, *dun-dun-dun*. The anticipation in my bones was exhilarating.

The moon was glowing brightly. The craters were so deep, five double-decker buses wouldn't fill them. Other planets were swarming in the sun in sync, one after another. The eerie sound of silence. It was pitch-black. All there was, was glowing stars and the Earth in the distance. It felt like being rocked around in a boat, side to side, without any balance and a chance of falling.

Raheem Ogwu (10)
Allen Edwards Primary School, Stockwell

Antarctica

I walked through the magic door, seeing lots and lots of snow piled on the floor as more snow kept coming. As I continued my journey, there were many trees in my way. They were all dead due to the cold.

As much more snow fell from the sky, I started getting frostbite. I knew I had to keep moving or I would freeze. More time passed and I started moving very slowly. It started to snow even harder and I was starting to lose hope.

As I kept on walking, I encountered a large polar bear that was looking at me. The second it did, I ran back to the magic door as I knew that thing could eat me. I managed to get back in through the door and I'll never go through a magic door again!

Chloe Chen (10)
Allen Edwards Primary School, Stockwell

Was It All A Dream On Planet Marble?

It all started when I was on my phone, watching TikTok. I was drinking a fresh glass of orange juice when a magical door appeared. It said, "Open me!" in a ghostly voice.

I opened the door and saw this blue and purple illusion. I went back in time to the late 1400s. In this place, there was gold sand scattered across the floor. Linicorns with tiger feet, a unicorn body, and lion head. And Tigersaurs, unicorn feet, dinosaur body, and tiger head.

There was a huge blue river that was called Crystal River. It led to a huge purple crystal. Magical plants lay over the gold dust. The place was covered in gold, purple, pink, blue, and green.

Miron Fenty (10)
Allen Edwards Primary School, Stockwell

Our Future Fate

I opened the door and it took me to an abandoned, deserted planet. There was a sound of low rumbling in my ears.

All around me was a rubbish wasteland. It smelt like an ancient rubbish dump. The land was covered in plastic wrappers. I could barely see the ground surface. Could this be our future fate?

What used to be rivers were now craters filled with cans and garbage bags. Old buildings resembled landmarks, shattered and covered with mould and litter.

Out of the corner of my eye, I noticed something glimmering. It almost blinded me. A golden, sparkling something...

Chanel Adewole (10)

Allen Edwards Primary School, Stockwell

The Spooky Haunted House

My magic door is very broken and bloody and has small cracks through it. The door is blood-curdling. As I proceed toward the door, my heart thumps. The door comes into view in a cemetery, behind a gravestone.

When the petrifying door opens, I see the inside of a house. Out of the corner of my eye, I see a shadow gazing down at me while I am touring the haunted house.

Suddenly, I feel that the shadow is behind me. Goosebumps descend down my arms. I hear bangs on the wall. As soon as it stops, there are footsteps and whistling.

Mouna Guendouz (9)
Allen Edwards Primary School, Stockwell

Wolf Land

I stepped through a mystical door with trees surrounding it, with branches like a wolf and a circle that looked like the moon. There was a black wolf with fire flaming around like an aura. The wolf stared at me like I was its prey.

Instead, it approached me with no hesitation and dragged me by my shirt. It led me to a strange wolf that was half white and half black. It had blue eyes and was as big as a tree. It seemed to be injured and looked very weak.

The black wolf nudged me, like they wanted me to cure it. So I did.

Bethel Ogiku (10)

Allen Edwards Primary School, Stockwell

The Sandy Beach And The Private Villa

As I walked down the hot, sandy beach, the sand swallowed me and led me to a private villa where I took a dip in the crystal, blue ocean as the breathtaking sunset slowly diminished.

As the next day arrived, the birds were chirping, the palm trees dancing, waves slowly crashing into the shore. I felt the cold water brushing my feet and the hot air brushing my hair.

As I put my hand through the water, there was a glimmer and sparkle as a little gold fish swam casually through the light-blue, crystal, glimmering ocean.

Anaiyah Bayliss (9)

Allen Edwards Primary School, Stockwell

Atlantis

I opened the door and there was a splash. There was an old wreck under the sea. From the corner of my eye, tropical, colourful fish were swarming me like bees.

My mouth could taste the salt and my hands could feel the silky sand. Fish made bubbles and when they popped, my ears flinched at the sound. My nose twitched at the smell of seaweed and coral. Everything felt peaceful and the coral reef was as bright as the sun. The sand felt as if it was too good to be true. It was so tranquil that nothing could disturb me.

Afeef Jurna (10)
Allen Edwards Primary School, Stockwell

The Magic Door

The vibrant mystery door appeared in the distance, standing there like a statue. As I approached the secret, chaotic door, there were salty baby-blue waves crashing down on the golden sand. It was unwinding and peaceful, the trees were dancing with their tropical leaves swaying around. The smell of coconuts twirled around my nose like a ballerina. The playful, blinding sand lay on the floor. The warm air brushed against my cheek. There were small bubbles coming up from the water. The shining, bright seashells swam up to me.

Bellange Eli Kya N'zeza (9)
Allen Edwards Primary School, Stockwell

The Magic Door

The dull, bloody door appeared from the darkness, waiting for its owner to come. As I drew closer to the door, it started to fade into an old, rusty version of itself.

Once I got to it, it creaked open by itself and a dark mist peeped out of the door. Then bats came flying out, some with injured wings. Once I stepped in, I could see bloody handprints scattered on the walls.

When I got outside, I could feel the damp, cold air. I could also feel a shiver down my spine as goosebumps travelled up my body.

Lola Brown (9)
Allen Edwards Primary School, Stockwell

Insomnia

I got up. *This*, I thought, *is going to be a normal day*. I saw that my door was made of sparkling cubes, but that was irrelevant to my exhausted brain.

I opened the door and fell into the abyss. "Oh, this is interesting." I was so tired, it sounded like a fish eating a biscuit.

When I hit the wooden floor, my instincts kicked in. My right arm was in agony, so I screamed for a bit. Well, not all of my instincts kicked in, but I noticed there was a door I could go through...

Harry Wood (10)

Allen Edwards Primary School, Stockwell

Ocean Adventure

I opened the door and was taken to the crystal-clear ocean. The sound of whale noises made me feel tranquil and delighted. The tiny, gentle waves overlapped each other, over and over again.
The peaceful snoring of the animals in their quiet sleep. The fish were chatting while the coral was swaying below them. The hungry sharks were hunting for playful fish. The jellyfish were using their tentacles to sting and eat their prey.
The water splashing on my toes made me feel relaxed and joyful.

Jazmine Price (9)
Allen Edwards Primary School, Stockwell

The Abandoned Dimension

With shaking hands, I opened the door and walked inside. The place was very gloomy. The sky was as grey as the moon.
In the corner of my eye, there were cracking, filthy houses moving side to side in a creepy alleyway. The clouds were moving depressingly. Banging and creaking sounds could be heard from a mile away. There was a shiver climbing down my spine. I was terrified. A strong breeze swiftly brushed down my shoulders.

Victoria Nkromah (9)
Allen Edwards Primary School, Stockwell

Space

The magic door looked colourful with lots of colours. It was old and it was made of wood. It was hard.

When I went in through the door, I was on the moon. It was big and grey and had craters. No one was there.

Then there was a spaceship that came. It looked old and silver and very dirty. After I made friends with the alien, we had a picnic.

Kallie (10)
Allen Edwards Primary School, Stockwell

The Evil Leprechaun

I found a strange door in my attic. It looked brand new, but I had never been in my attic before so I didn't know. The door looked magical and if it was a human, it would probably be kind and friendly. So I opened it and found myself in a beautiful field of flowers. All of a sudden, a shiver ran down my spine.

Daisy-May Norfield (11)
Allen Edwards Primary School, Stockwell

The Magic Door

A mythical door emerged in front of me. It took me to Antarctica. The atmosphere around was cold and frozen. Crunching ice after every step echoed through the valley. A big wave of salt water arrived and took ice with it. Wind was blowing in my face. It was so cold in the Antarctic, I could barely breathe.

Jordan Orum (9)
Allen Edwards Primary School, Stockwell

The Magical Door

The thunderstruck amethyst door stood as it waited for its prey. As I approached the sapphire door handle, lightning flashed before my eyes. The underwater city's buildings glimmered in the sparkling, diamond water. The seaweed waved as I passed by. Soundwaves travelled through the air.

Jenavi Diegbe
Allen Edwards Primary School, Stockwell

The Basketball Adventure

I was playing basketball with my friends when the basketball got caught in the hoop. I couldn't reach it, so I had to ask my friends to give me a boost. By a boost, I mean a little boost. My friends put their hands out in front of me and with all their strength, they gave me a little boost. That was all I needed.

So I reached up and swung up onto the hoop. You'd think I'd just grab it and get down, but no! I fell down through the basket and that was when I thought some magic was about to become undone.

I found myself in a place that looked like Mars on the ground but on the top and sides, it was pitch-black. All I could see was my future self and Elon Musk. He threw his controller at me because he lost the game. The aliens started to scream, "Why? Why? Why?"

Riley Lawson (8)
Forehill Primary School, Bridge Of Don

The Wonderful Place

Once upon a time, there was a girl called Hallee. Hallee was in her car when, in the distance, she saw an awesome castle. Hallee got out of her car. She walked and walked until she got to it and went inside.

She found the person from Matilda. She raced over and gave Matilda a huge hug. It turned out she was in Christmas Disney World. They ran out and, surprisingly, all the Matilda characters were there. She had never been happier!

Hallee threw her arms around Matilda. All the characters - except for Miss Trunchbull - had a big group hug. Hallee looked at her watch and said, "I'm sorry, guys, but I have to go. It's getting late and it's going to get dark. I'll see you another time, I promise."

"That's fine," said Matilda.

Tilly Lloyd-Ogg (8)
Forehill Primary School, Bridge Of Don

Raimart Planet

Once upon a time, a girl called Melissa moved to a beautiful new home but she didn't like it. She had a giant argument with her mum, so she went upstairs to her awful, scratched bedroom door.
It flew right open and then she saw a place full of sweets! It was Raimart Planet. She ran straight through the doorway. She started to eat happily but hadn't realised the door had disappeared! When the king heard about this, he wasn't happy at all. But this little guy with no nose or legs, called Mark, warned Melissa. She ran as fast as she could to the place where the door was, but the door wasn't there.
Mark, the little marshmallow, gave her a sticky wand. She wished to be home, then found herself outside her beautiful new home.

Melissa Rodgers (8)
Forehill Primary School, Bridge Of Don

The Magic Door

I saw a magic door. I went through it and it led to space. In space, I saw the sun and felt the air. But there was no air in space!

I was going into the sun and it was too hot in there. I saw the Sun King and he said, "You are not the king in the sun." I said I knew that I was not the king. The king said, "You stole my gold."

I said, "No, I did not steal your gold."

"Fine! You did not steal my gold," the king said. "You go away."

I said, "Okay, okay, I will go away."

Then I got out and the door was locked. I was locked in space! The Sun King had a war and the door was unlocked. I ran and ran, and the Sun King went into the sun.

Kayden Grace (8)
Forehill Primary School, Bridge Of Don

The Adventures In Candy Land

Once upon a time, there was a little boy called Alex. Alex had black hair, a blue top, and ripped jeans. One day, Alex was walking home from school and he spotted a rusty metal door.

He said to himself, "That door has never been there before." He walked closer to the door and pushed it open. It creaked and, suddenly, Alex got sucked into the doorway.

Alex found himself in a land full of candy. There were Mars bar magpies, and gummies, sweets, and more. Alex thought he was dreaming but he found out he was not. He thought it was so amazing, he decided to explore the world full of candy.

Faith Spicer (8)
Forehill Primary School, Bridge Of Don

The Magic Door

Once upon a time, there was a person called Harrison. Harrison went into the attic and found a mysterious, old door. Harrison decided to go in the creaky old door and found his little brother, James. He was able to talk! Harrison was amazed. He could talk!

But then Harrison realised that they were floating in space. Then Harrison saw a floating house and outside the house, there was a baby Yoda shooting an alien with a gun. Then Harrison and James heard big stomping and gunshots. They felt tickly, cold, and they couldn't feel their bodies.

Harrison Beattie (8)

Forehill Primary School, Bridge Of Don

The Unknown Aliens

I was in the woods when I saw a glowing thing. I approached it and I saw an advanced, hovering, metal door. I saw a button so I pressed it.

The door made a horrible screeching sound when it opened. I went through it and saw green, slimy, big-headed, bald aliens with four arms, red eyes, and horns as big as hands.

I saw spaceships as big as buses and buildings as big as skyscrapers. I went closer to a colossal building. I spotted guards. I knew there was something important in there. I didn't know what would happen next.

Oliver He (8)
Forehill Primary School, Bridge Of Don

Santa's Workshop

I walked up to my room but I saw something. It was a big fancy door. I went in. It led me to a snowy and cold place. I saw somebody. They had red on and were with some people that had green on.

I followed them. They took me to this workshop. I realised the guy dressed in green was Buddy. They saw me. Santa said, "Who are you?"

I said, "I'm Ramona." But I also said, "I see Mrs Claus." She gave me a cookie, they were so good. I went on a sleigh ride. I was so excited to go on some more.

Ramona Sinclair (8)
Forehill Primary School, Bridge Of Don

Lollipop Land

Once upon a time, Allie went through the sparkly, brown magic door. It took her to Lollipop Land.
Allie saw Queen Layla, Queen of Lollipop Land. She said, "Who are you?"
Allie said, "My name is Allie."
Layla said, "There is a delicious lollipop shop just around the corner."
So Allie got back with her rainbow lollipop and lived happily ever after.

Allie Massie (8)
Forehill Primary School, Bridge Of Don

The Magic Door

Behind the door, the unicorns were looking at the moon through the window and saw shooting stars and gold fireworks. The fireworks were loud but the unicorns were fine with noise.

The fireworks were for the king. The magic was sparkling and rainbows. They were celebrating Christmas. They played music that was loud. The last person to enter the land became king.

Grayson Deans (8)
Forehill Primary School, Bridge Of Don

The Magic Door

I was walking in the forest when I saw a door in a tree. I opened the door and I went inside. I saw a weird animal. It looked like a Pokémon. I saw a city and I heard another Pokémon.

I was walking in a field. I saw my friend. I said, "Do you know the way out?"

He said, "Yes, follow me," and I was home.

Jayden Morgan (9)

Forehill Primary School, Bridge Of Don

The Magic Door

Once upon a time, there was a boy called Kevin
and he saw a potion that could make you smaller.
He drank it. He shrank! Then he saw a door
opening into his body and he went inside. Then the
door was gone. It was screechy. Inside the body
were blood bubbles and it was all red. He
wondered what would be next.

Kevin Busch (8)
Forehill Primary School, Bridge Of Don

The T-Rex Attack

Hi, my name is Elias and I'm eight. My story begins on a day I was going to my friend's house. I went to my bedroom but when I opened the door, a vortex was there! I got sucked in and I landed on a T-rex! I was confused. I wondered when I would get home.

Elias Broche (8)
Forehill Primary School, Bridge Of Don

The Magic Door

One day, me and my wonderful family moved house. One week later, when I was in bed, reading, I saw a mysterious light coming from outside. So I looked out of my window to see where it came from. Out of the corner of my eye, I saw a beautiful door!

I went downstairs and went to the beautiful door. I opened the door and, suddenly, I was in a scrumptious world! Everything was candy, what a smell! I could hear a lot of chatting and, of course, a lot of munching, and sounds like machines making all sorts of candy.

I could see lots of gingerbread people and chocolate fountains and toffee chairs and goodness knew what else! I could feel the warmth of the toasted marshmallow squishiness of gigantic marshmallows. They were used for pillows and beds!

After a lot of looking around, a kind gingerbread man said, "Come into my house, young man."

I replied, "Thank you, your house looks really nice."

He replied, "Thank you!"

So I spent five hours with my new friend and thought, *I should really go home now.* I said goodbye and that I would come another time. I went through the door and thought to myself, *it's good to be home, though.*

Brady Schols (8)
Greenfields School, Forest Row

The Magic Door

I stepped through a door and found myself in... space! I was so confused. Was I dreaming? I went in, suddenly my body started to float. It was uncontrollable. Soon enough, I got the hang of it. I looked around, it was beautiful. I wanted to explore, but space could be dangerous so I just wobbled to a nearby planet. I was wandering around, then, in a flash, something caught my eye. Suddenly, a monster arose in front of me. It had four eyes, one leg, and fifty arms!

It started to chase me. We ran around and around the planet. Then I thought and thought, and I knew what I had to do. I crouched down and leapt through space and to the magic door. The monster was right there... I shut the door as fast as I could! I said to myself, "That was fun, but also scary. Maybe I'll do it again and see where I end up next."

Logan Beyer (10)
Greenfields School, Forest Row

The Magic Door

Once upon a time, on a normal day, I found an unusual door that looked like it was glued onto the tree. When I went inside, it was a completely different world! There were candy canes, Christmas trees, and more. There was snow everywhere too. I was worried because I didn't know how to go back to get the jacket and the gloves. Then I remembered I had a sweater so I decided to wear it. Snow started falling and, by mistake, I tasted the snow and I was surprised, it tasted so much like sugar! I realised it was a magical day of my life.

Even if I was all by myself, I enjoyed it a lot. I wasn't really by myself since there were gingerbread dogs, candy cane birds, and vanilla cats. I had a good time, but eventually, the portal opened and I was thrown back home. This would be the most unforgettable day of my life.

Vishakha Mishra (11)
Greenfields School, Forest Row

The Magic Door

I stepped through the magic door and I found... my school! I was flabbergasted. I looked around, no one was there. I walked around and started to figure out where I was. I was in the junior hall locker room.

"Okay," I said to myself. Then I started to walk over to Mr Bones' maths room. I looked around and spotted someone else. It was not a normal person though, it was a stickman-like figure and had no head.

Then the bell rang and a whole lot of them came flooding in. I heard zombie-like moaning sounds coming from them. I was scared, so I ran down the gloomy corridor and went to where the door was last. It was gone!

I whipped myself around and saw all of the dead-like students following me. I knew that was the last of me.

Cassidy McEntyre (10)
Greenfields School, Forest Row

The Corridor

I opened the magic door and saw a brightly illuminated corridor. The corridor was glowing with bright purple LED lights. At the end of the corridor, there were two doors.

One of the doors had a sign next to it that said: *Aliens*, it was neon yellow. The other door looked the same, but the sign said: *Humans*. From the 'alien'-labelled door, there came a small popping sound that gave me goosebumps. From the 'human'-labelled door, I heard a relaxing humming. The floor was very cold and yet the walls were hot. I also felt a tugging sensation in my stomach. Now came the big decision: which door? I obviously chose the alien door.

Flora Huszar (11)
Greenfields School, Forest Row

Candyland World Cup

Earlier today I was in the park when I stumbled across a magic door. There were sparkles all around the door and I could hear cheering from the other side.

Once I got through the door, I plonked onto a seat and started to look around. *Where am I?* I thought to myself. *Wait, I know! I'm at Wembley!*

I looked around a bit more and saw that everything was seemingly made of sweets and chocolate, so I grabbed some toffee off the seat next to mine because I had the whole row to myself.

The game ended 7-0 to England! After, I found the magic door. I stumbled back through and told Mum everything!

Finlay Bennett (9)

Greenfields School, Forest Row

Roblox

I found a door, then I opened the door and I found Roblox. I played Roblox Doors and Doors kicked me out to the Noob Army.

I went into Minecraft and I saw Noob Army again. They threw me in the Noob jail. Then I escaped the Noob jail and I found diamonds and a skeleton killed me.

I went in Among Us. Red was acting sus. I followed Red and I found Red next to a dead body. I voted for Red, Red was the imposter. We won.

I was a Stikman and I stole a bike and listened to music. The police were following me and I crashed. I was on max level and did left, down, up, up, right, up.

Gabbi Sipos (8)
Greenfields School, Forest Row

The World Of Alisa

Once upon a time, there was a girl named Alisa. One day, Alisa found a door. It was made of metal and had lots of pink flowers.

She went through the door and saw foxes running on a purple field with a beautiful green sky. She saw pepperoni dripping off pizza trees and super soft cotton candy bushes. She was so amazed by this amazing world.

She had so much fun. She went there every day after school and she never told anyone about the magical place.

Alisa Krasnyakova (9)
Greenfields School, Forest Row

The Big Cuddly Bear And The Elves

I went through the magic door. First, I saw a bear and she was super kind. She invited me to tea. She let me call her Grandma.

She loved children. We went for walks together and she was the boss of the machinery factory. She let me go with her. She knew I loved machinery. The elves greeted me and I helped.

It was a great, great time with her. And I would see her soon!

Oscar Wysocki (9)

Greenfields School, Forest Row

Winter Wonderland

I went through the magic door and it was pyjama day. I found myself in Winter Wonderland. It was freezing!

I could smell cake. I could hear deer running and I could see snow falling. It was so magnificent. A deer came over and it showed me around.

That was the best day ever. I didn't want to leave but I did because I would miss my family.

Alexa Halasz (9)

Greenfields School, Forest Row

Racing Land

One day, I found a magic door. I went through it and saw a man. He gave me a car. He told me that I was called to participate in a race.
All of a sudden, I was in a race. It was so scary, but I won. Then I went on a dirtbike. I fell so many times but it was fun. Now it was time to go home.

Quentin Garcia (8)
Greenfields School, Forest Row

The Land Of Fire

One day, I saw a door in the attic. I went through it and something amazing happened. I was taken to a land of fire!

I could see lava everywhere and flying dragons. I could hear volcanoes erupting and volcanic rocks crumbling.

When I came back, I thought, *I want to go back!*

Ivar Van De Visch (9)
Greenfields School, Forest Row

A Talking Panda In China

My teacher showed me a door. She said, "Go in!"
I went in and I was in a bamboo forest. I saw a
panda that could talk. Then I ran to it and hugged
it.
I will never tell anyone because I would like to be
alone with my panda friend.

Alice Contu (9)

Greenfields School, Forest Row

The Elven Door

One rainy day, I climbed slowly into the loft in search of something to do when I came across a small door. I turned the handle and cautiously stepped over the threshold. I found myself on the edge of a bustling village! Even better, it was a Lego elves village - but life-size! All the characters were moving and chatting.

I walked toward a girl and she said, "I haven't seen you before, what's your name? Mine is Mya." She had a lovely smile.

"Hi, my name is Layla," I replied.

Me and Mya became friends and I also found out we were the same age. She showed me around the area, introduced me to everyone, and showed me how to bond with the animals. There was a beautiful black panther who took a liking to me, she was called Shakira.

Me and Mya spent hours exploring, with Shakira and Luka (a monkey) accompanying us. We sat in Mya's treehouse and chatted. Day after day, I would disappear to the elven village. Also, whenever I went back home, it would be the same time as when I left.

We went swimming, fishing, tree climbing, mountain climbing, and fruit picking. I bonded with Shakira and rode her when we defended the village from the evil goblins. When I grew up, I let my kids in on the secret.

Amalia St Pierre (10)

Heamoor Community Primary School, Heamoor

Jerry's Magical Door

One evening, I was bored like never before. I was so bored, I didn't even want to eat (that was very unusual for me). I was banging my head against the wall, thinking of what to do. Suddenly, I saw a tiny little door.

Without thinking, I ran to the door. I wanted to investigate. As I started opening the door, I shrank. I didn't care much because I was focusing on getting inside and exploring.

Slowly, I crept in. I could see a tiny bed, a cooker, another tiny little door, and some cartons of milk. I'd never seen this type of milk before. I could hear some loud clapping noises in the background. I could also hear something cracking. Because of the noises, I went to the other door.

I walked in. It opened up into a world full of water, strangely, I could breathe. There was a mouse staring at me. How could the mouse breathe? He told me to walk back into the other room. He told me his name was Jerry. I followed him back to the other room.

As soon as I sat down, he started shouting at me. He told me to get out. I still couldn't quite make out what those noises were, but I knew I would be going back soon.

Tyler Dale (10)

Heamoor Community Primary School, Heamoor

Spooky Scary Cereals

One cold, rainy night, while everyone was sleeping, I was awake. Instead of trying to get back to sleep like a normal, boring person would, I stayed up, wandering around the house, trying to find something, anything! A monster, a door, even a ghost, anything really.

I had been living in this house for a year and was already bored until I found a great but terrifying discovery that ended with everyone in my household in hospital. Every other day, I used to search my house back to front, trying to find something. One night, I went and got a ladder and went into the loft. I'd been told not to go in there, but I was curious so I went in with no second thoughts.

In the room, I saw a big pile of toys, books, and teddies with loads of spoons and cereal boxes. I uncovered a box and saw a big brass door handle. I pulled on it and all of the stuff fell on the floor just enough that I could get in. I got in. There was a big room with small pieces of cereal holding spoons like they were knives...

Alexander Davy Eddy (10)

Heamoor Community Primary School, Heamoor

The Jungle Door

Josh was running from his dog, Leo, when he saw a tiny door in the wall. "Ah, I better go in there to get away from Leo." He got in and there were stairs. He ran up them because he thought Leo might still be chasing him. When he got to the top, he opened a blue door.

"Woah!" Josh had walked into a forest. Then the door slammed. "*Aah!*" screamed Josh.

"No need to scream, bro. It's just a door. I'm Thomas, I'm also a monkey," said Thomas.

"Oh, sorry. I'm Josh, nice to meet you," said Josh.

"Cool," said Thomas. "Come with me, I'll take you to see my friends."

"Okay," said Josh as they walked off into the woods.

"Hi!" they all said. There were eight of them. "Let me show you around," said one. "This is our bedroom, this is our food-cooking place..."

"Wait, I need to go home," said Josh. "Bye!"

Grace Gould (10)

Heamoor Community Primary School, Heamoor

The Magic Door

One sunny morning, there was a magic door. It looked like a normal door. It was so small that I couldn't fit in it. I was so confused. Nervously, I opened it and, all of a sudden, there was a box with a lot of blood and it had teeth! It looked at me and I slammed the door on him before he could bite me.

Slowly, the door opened again and I ran as fast as I could to get away. But he was hot on my heels. Then there was a toy on the floor and I threw it at him. I ran to mine and my brother's room and slammed the door in his face. He struggled to get back up. Then he ran back to his door and went back to eating people.

I went to tell Mum and Dad so I could show them the door, but the door wasn't there. When they left, it was back. I opened it and there was another box. I shouted for Mum and Dad but the TV was so loud. I started to panic and the two boxes started chasing me. I ran to the front room and they weren't there. I heard chatting in the kitchen...

Jacob Rendall (10)
Heamoor Community Primary School, Heamoor

The Door That Had Never Been Opened

Many moons ago, I awoke to the loud noises of bashing and banging. It was so annoying. I wasn't sure what to do at this point, it was very scary. But Mum always said, "Don't be silly, it's our lovely house, no one could come in!"

I ran faster than the speed of light from my front room to my kitchen and skidded across the floor. I came to a big pile of pancakes with syrup. I couldn't help but eat some.

The door pinged open, it was full of goblins and singing slugs. Trembling with fear, I said, "Hello," politely.

They replied, "*Helloo*, we're the singing sludwas, short for singing slugs and dwarfs. If there is something you hate or don't like, it will appear. Also, everyone that has entered hasn't again."

All the things I disliked were there, like everything healthy. All the sludwas laughed at me, so I slammed the door in their faces and locked it with the rusty old lock, and never returned.

Honey Prowse (10)

Heamoor Community Primary School, Heamoor

The Hidden Birthday Present

One rainy Sunday, I was trapped inside because of the horrible weather. I was bored. I was sitting quietly, thinking of what I could possibly do when, all of a sudden, in the corner of my eye, I caught a glimpse of a tiny door about a third of the size of a normal door. It was part of the wall, almost as if it was a miniature storage compartment.

I thought to myself, *what could possibly be in there?* I approached the door and I heard weird, video-game-like music and beeping from inside. I pulled the metallic handle and I could not believe my eyes - it was a spacious arcade and football pitch!

I wriggled through the tiny door and tried to find a game. It said on the bit where you put your coin in: 'one token needed', so I grabbed a pot full of tokens and played some games. Then I went over and played football for a while. Then my mum called me. I told her about it and then she said it was meant for my birthday tomorrow! "Oh!" I said.

Harry Thomson (10)
Heamoor Community Primary School, Heamoor

Magic Is Real

Early one morning, I was on a walk in my local forest when I saw a door. It was on a tree and it seemed to be glowing a luscious yellowy light. I was intrigued so I went over and opened it.

I felt a warm glow on my face. I cautiously walked in. I came out in an abandoned, wrecked city, as if it was in an apocalypse. Suddenly, these people in druid clothes started gathering around me, saying, "You must be the prophecy!"

"We must teach him magic!" shouted another. "To help us fight!"

"Magic? But magic isn't real," I said.

"Just you wait and see," said their leader.

After days of practise, I had learnt magic. Magic pulsed and vibrated through me. They trained me so I could fight the mutant plants. Sounds crazy, right? Well, I did it. I cut, slashed, jumped, and hooked until I had finished my job - just in time for tea.

Zethar Savage (10)
Heamoor Community Primary School, Heamoor

The 1800s

In my small home, I found a door. A door I hadn't discovered before. It had twirly, whirly lines on it, spinning around in a mesmerising pattern. I felt the small cracks in its cold texture, just convincing me to open it. *Should I open it?*

With trembling hands, I opened the door. After that, I stepped into a cold, dark world. No light, just dark. There were people in old, ragged dresses. No! The 1800s! I couldn't bear it. There were old shops, horrible people, small narrow cobbled roads that were full of people.

I could hear awful people saying rude things to others, the slight trot of heels against the cold road. I felt awful and disgusted, cold, sad, lonely, and hurt. What was I to do? Run away? Then I spotted a door on a shop. It looked the same as my old door. I ran to it, nudged it, and jumped through. I was home, all safe, and oh my, I needed it!

Aimee Maddern (10)
Heamoor Community Primary School, Heamoor

Candy Cane Door

Once, there was a girl called Lucy and her dog called Poppy. Poppy loved the woods, so she took Poppy to the woods. When they got there, Poppy zoomed out of the car and Lucy ran after her and caught her staring at an oak tree.

Lucy looked around. There was a door. It had a picture of a candy cane on it. She went inside and it looked like a candy land. She was speechless. There were fluffy cotton candy clouds and a river made of melted ice cream. The sand on the beach was lemon sherbert, the sea was syrup, and lollipop flowers and gummy bears were bouncing around.

This man came up to her and said, "'Ello, mate, are you lost?"

"No," said Lucy. "Where am I?"

"You, my friend, are in Sweet City..."

Mylee Reynolds (11)

Heamoor Community Primary School, Heamoor

The Christmas Door Adventure

I was walking in a jungle, very deep in the jungle, and came across a door. What was it doing there? It had snow in front of it and slight cracks on it. A strange door, it was. I touched the door and it glowed gold and red! "It must be magic!" I said to myself.

I opened the door and saw loads of snow and very tall Christmas trees covered in snow. Candy canes were growing tall and there were animals that were living their best lives. I could hear children's laughter echoing from far away, so I decided to follow the noise.

A kid talked to me. "I'm lost!" the kid cried.

"Oh no!" I said to him.

I found out that he was on holiday and his parents went home without him. I decided to adopt him and go back home.

Cherry-Mae O'keife (9)

Heamoor Community Primary School, Heamoor

The Magic Safari

One day, when I stepped out of my house, there was a strange brown door with branches over it. I had never seen this weird door before. I opened the door and there was a man wearing a jungle suit and circular glasses. He was stood about 1.5m away from the door.

He welcomed me in, telling me where I was and what there was to do. When I walked through all of the leaves, all of the animals stared at me. They all stood there. The man next to me started growling and chest-beating. At the same time, he started talking 'animal'.

It was getting late and dark and it was time to start heading back home. I was enjoying myself, it was fun. I told them I would visit tomorrow. So I walked back and jumped through the door.

Mason Ziwange (9)
Heamoor Community Primary School, Heamoor

The African Adventure

One day, I found a magic door. I went through it and found a hot summer day in Africa! In Africa, I was on one of the beaches. I could see people having the best time ever, splashing in the gentle water. It looked like so much fun.

When I was standing in the sand, I was rummaging my feet through the sand. It was hot and the softest thing I had ever felt. Suddenly, two people started arguing. I couldn't believe it. Everyone went silent.

When the people were arguing, a little girl came up and said, "Can you stop this?"

"Sorry, no," I said.

When I was walking toward the door, it had disappeared so I couldn't get back!

Willow Trevail (8)

Heamoor Community Primary School, Heamoor

The Sand Monsters

I was having a nice walk on the beach. I heard a loud bang and I walked on something hard, so I started digging. After a long time, I hit a door. A mysterious, black door. I was afraid.

I opened the door and banged my head on the ground. I opened my eyes and saw ten sandcastles floating in the air. I said, "Hello."

They looked at me, then the open door, and said, "Man! A man! Kill him." They ran after me and got me. They stuck me to a wall with sticky sand.

They stared at me and one of them said, "Shall we eat him?"

"Yes," said another. "I think he is dangerous, we should eat him."

Zachary Timings (10)

Heamoor Community Primary School, Heamoor

The Magic Jungle Door

Upon arriving at my new house, I saw a door. The door was locked and then I found out it was a magic door. My parents couldn't see it!

The next day, I tried opening the door again and it was unlocked. I went inside and saw a jungle, but it wasn't just any ordinary jungle, it was a magic jungle! There were funny-looking animals as well. Suddenly, I heard something and as soon as I looked up, there was a monkey shouting, "Look out!"

When it landed on my face, my body started to tingle. Suddenly, I went back to my house and the door disappeared. It was a fun adventure but I was happy to be home.

Libby Cringle (9)
Heamoor Community Primary School, Heamoor

Adventure In Cat Land

One afternoon, I was bored so I decided to go through the mysterious door with cats on it. I was so glad I went through it! Everywhere there was cat-themed stuff. I stayed for a week!

In that time, something strange happened. A big dog appeared, scaring the cats! The dog said, "If you want me to go, you must find the Dog Land key and give it to me." This scared the cats.

The king cat, Bob, made a speech. Me and some cats would go into the deep, dark cave. Some days later, we found the key! We gave it to the dog so he could go home. After that, I went home. I wanted to go back to Cat Land every week!

Daisy Coates (8)

Heamoor Community Primary School, Heamoor

Nyan Cat Adventures Around The World

Once upon a time, there was a kid named Isla and she found a door. She went through it and she found herself rolling down a hill. She stood up and she wasn't herself, she was... Nyan Cat!

Isla said, "OMG! I'm Nyan Cat!" She saw Sports Cat. Nyan Cat raced toward Sports Cat and did her power-up which went like this, "*Miiaoow! Miaooow! Miaoow!*"

Sports Cat said, "Oh no!" Before he could say Nyan Cat, he was launched into Candy Land. And Isla went through the door and went home.

Isla-Grace Walker (9)
Heamoor Community Primary School, Heamoor

Vikings

One night, a little girl went deep into the forest and she saw a big checkered door. She decided to go through it.

She suddenly woke up on this weird bed. There wasn't a proper light, but there was a lantern. She saw some stairs so she got out of bed and walked up the stairs.

She was on a Viking longship. There were two people fighting with massive swords. She was so scared, she ran back down. Luckily, the checkered door was under the boat. She went through, back to the forest, but she was never seen again.

Emilie Marshall (9)
Heamoor Community Primary School, Heamoor

The Magic Door

I looked up and saw a magic door in the sky. Luckily for me, I had my jetpack. I opened the door and found myself in a land of dinosaurs.

I was scared because I saw the dinosaurs fighting. They were knocking down trees and making big holes with their feet. The ground was shaking and I didn't know what to do.

A man shot at the dinosaurs, killing one and injuring the other. I used my jetpack to go back through the door. When I landed back home, I noticed there was a baby dinosaur hiding on my jetpack.

Ethan Billinger (9)
Heamoor Community Primary School, Heamoor

Into The Future

I was walking through a jungle, but when I turned right, I saw a mysterious door covered in vines and leaves. When I walked through the door, I was in the future and there were cars hovering above me. Other people were time travelling back 200 years. There were people in cars staring at me because I was from the past. I could see buildings with bright blue lights coming from inside. The lights came out of the windows.

A few hours later, after exploring, I went back through the door into the jungle.

Riley Buckingham (10)
Heamoor Community Primary School, Heamoor

The Magic Door

One night, in a forest, I found a glowing door.
There were so many colours!
I went through the door and discovered a new galaxy. I didn't know which one.
the air was silent.
I saw mysterious red creatures with three legs and weird spaceships and boats. There was a boat that could travel through space!
We did ten laps around the planet and then went back through the door. We were back in the forest.
I decided to go home and have dinner before going back to explore.

Morgan Buckingham (10)
Heamoor Community Primary School, Heamoor

Into Space

One day, a girl named Pearl was walking her dog down to the forest. As she was walking, she found a door that was changing colours, purple to black to white to blue. Pearl was very curious, so she went in.

As she slowly tiptoed in through the colourful door, she brought her dog. Juno started barking and getting scared. Pearl calmed Juno down and started to explore.

A blaring light appeared, so Pearl ran back out to the forest and went home and came back the next day.

Ruby Spencer (9)
Heamoor Community Primary School, Heamoor

The Purple Swirl Door

I stepped through a swirly, purple door that I found in the forest and I found myself in a fun animal centre. I saw silly monkeys swinging on the vines and lions yawning. The animals were play-fighting as well as running around.

I could hear the lions roaring super loudly and the birds squawking. The breeze was amazing, it felt like I was in a jungle with the noise around me. I said to myself, "I should go back now." I jumped back to where I was before.

Amelie Furse (9)

Heamoor Community Primary School, Heamoor

The Scary, Dark, Deadly Land

I stepped into the scary, dark door and I was in a scary, dark place. When I was in there, I looked around. There were dead trees, lots of stuff. I heard a noise but I did nothing. I stood shocked because I saw a clown! Then I ran like never before.

The next day, I looked around again. I saw lots of snowy stuff. But then I saw the door. It was so amazing, but then a baby tiger came. It was hurt, so I took it home. We lived an amazing life.

Ziva Lang (8)

Heamoor Community Primary School, Heamoor

Jack Skeleton

I stepped through a door and found myself in a Christmas wonderland. I saw bright, beautiful Christmas lights and white fluffy snow. I could hear children singing loudly and cheerfully. I could feel the soft white snow.

I wandered around and I watched toys being made and Christmas lights being put up. Then Santa came and put me on his sleigh and I went back home. Santa's sleigh crashed into the door.

Lily Bawden-Bonell (8)
Heamoor Community Primary School, Heamoor

The Magic Door

Today, I found a magic door in the woods and it was on a tree. I went into it and it took me to a nice calm beach. I was so excited.

I took my shoes off and I could feel sand. It tickled my feet. I found a seashell and I could hear the sea. Then I walked to the side and saw some palm trees.

I went back through the magic door because it was time for me to go.

Jasmine Wright (9)
Heamoor Community Primary School, Heamoor

The Forest

One day, I walked in the forest. I saw a wolf lurking by the river. He was drinking water and the people were scared because when they went past the black wolf it was hunting for people.
Suddenly a big lion saved the people and there was a fight with the lion vs wolf. The wolf didn't die, then they hugged and then the wolf had a baby.

Niayah Wildman (8)

Heamoor Community Primary School, Heamoor

The Magic Door

One day, I found a wide, glowing door. I stopped and looked. I went through. I was in the sea! A jellyfish was heading toward me.

I panicked, I had no idea what to do. Then the door came. I swam through the door then I ended up at Hogwarts! I saw Harry Potter, Hermione, and Ron Weasley. They took me to the sorting room. I was a Ravenclaw!

Sophia Tonkin (9)

Heamoor Community Primary School, Heamoor

Mac And Cheese

I went through the door and all I could see was mac and cheese! There was no way out, the door shut behind me. I felt I was trapped forever.
All of a sudden, a bright light appeared from nowhere. I could smell and hear the cheese sizzling loudly. My tummy started rumbling. I was getting very hungry.

Logan Anderson (9)
Heamoor Community Primary School, Heamoor

The Beach

One day, two very lovely girls called Max and Phoebe had just found a big door. They opened it and there was a tropical island. It had the most beautiful sunset and sea and sand. It was beautiful. Soon, the sea came in and there was a storm. Then they went back.

Lizzie Strick (9)

Heamoor Community Primary School, Heamoor

Door

An extract

There were five of us on board. The others were asleep. Can you believe that, by the way? We were in a rocket, spinning hopelessly out of control and into forever, and their chosen course of action? A nap!

So, as they slept their sweet dreams, I was going crazy inside, worrying. It didn't help that two red emergency lights were flashing wildly like we were in some kind of disco party. How could they sleep? I swam to another part of the rocket. I was in the control room, where everything went wrong. Then I noticed this metal door I had never seen before. I realised it had a big wheel on it and a place where you put in a number code. It also had big bold letters: *Do Not Enter.*

I put a code in anyway. 1234, the only code I knew. Miraculously, somehow, it opened. I wished I thought things through more. I was sucked in. It was some type of portal, colourful blobs of planets passed me. Finally, after what felt like hours, I landed on an upside-down world.

First, I thought it was Australia, but there were no people. The tigers had elephant bodies. All the creatures had different bodies than they did on Earth. But some things were the same, there were still trees and flowers, but more colourful. I shouted into the dark forest, "I am going out into the wild, remember me if I don't come back!"

Darcey Mottram (10)

St Mary's Catholic Primary School, Broadway

The Magic Door

An extract

There were five of us on board. The others were asleep. Can you believe that, by the way? We were in a rocket, spinning hopelessly out of control and into forever, and their chosen course of action: a nap!
I decided to get out of bed. It was too uncomfortable. I sat down in a chair, looking at a farmer's house in a picture, until I realised that the door handle was not just 2D or part of the picture - it was real! It was real, 3D metal. I was sure it was a way home.
I pulled off the picture and found that I was facing a magenta door. I pulled it open and heard a high-pitched squeal which turned into an ear-splitting crack! I opened my eyes and squinted as all I could see was a very bright blue. I was on an enormous, blue planet.
That wasn't the only strange thing - there were small creatures. They looked cute and adorable, except I didn't realise that they hated humans!
One of them picked up what I figured was a radio. A screech exploded out of its mouth. Out of the blue, an invisible laser tore through the ground. Without warning, I heard water splashing.

All of the adorable aliens turned red and fangs popped out of their mouths. They faced me. I made a run for it, sprinting full-pace to the door which was counting down. 10, 9, 8... I had 5 seconds or I would be trapped forever!

Noah Skidmore (9)
St Mary's Catholic Primary School, Broadway

Liam And His Fairy Land

There were five of us on board. The others were asleep. Can you believe that, by the way? We were in a rocket, spinning hopelessly out of control and into forever, and their chosen course of action: a nap!

I chose to tour the rocket. First, I looked through the rectangular-shaped window and saw the stars glimmering in the dark blue sky. Next, I bounced to the front of the rocket where all the buttons were. I could hear an insistent beep.

I gambolled closer and tried to find which button was making the noise. Accidentally, I pressed a square-shaped button and it led me to a hatch that said, *No Entry* in black, bold, threatening letters. I unlocked the hatch and it led me to a shopping mall. It wasn't an ordinary shopping mall, it was a giant mall.

I was floating around when I realised that my best friend was beside me, not moving. I tried touching her but she didn't move, I tried kicking her and she didn't move, I tried shoving her and she still didn't move. The last thing, I knew would work: a smelly sock. Since the sock was so smelly, I fainted. And it all turned out to be a nightmare.

When I woke up from my horrible nightmare, I was in the rocket. I tried looking for the hatch but it was just a normal wall. Then I heard something, it was a bang. We had crashed.

Anna Sijo (10)
St Mary's Catholic Primary School, Broadway

Planet Earth?

An extract

There were only five of us and just me awake. The rest were sleeping. I still couldn't believe their decision to go to sleep while we were doomed in space. I was looking out, admiring all the stars, but I knew I had to do something before we ran out of oxygen.

I started to bring myself up and floated around the capsule, I had to have fun in zero gravity! Some time later, I was wondering if I could maybe get us back toward Earth, so I had to start floating around, looking at the metallic doors. I couldn't find a door with the words 'control room', so I had to open every single door.

The pitch-black handles were as cold as ice. I thought I would lose all my fingers. Most of the rooms were filled with sleeping bags or crates filled with supplies. Suddenly, I came across a flashy sign that was bright orange, saying, *Control Room*. I was so excited that we could go back home! Or so I thought.

As I got closer, the door got brighter and brighter until it opened by itself and I was sucked in. There were white beams of light taking me so fast, I couldn't feel a thing. I got worried but, in the distance, I saw something. It looked like a world, but with aliens. They were cheering and celebrating. They had a trophy in their hands and I was going to grab it when I flew past.

Oscar Ford (11)
St Mary's Catholic Primary School, Broadway

Liam's Magic Door

A nap! We were endlessly flying through space on a billion-pound rocket and guess what? They were asleep! While I was alone, I might as well have a look around. I came up to this room with millions of flashing lights. I was flying around the room when I noticed something: a hatch!

I opened the hatch and crawled through. Halfway through, parts of the crawlspace were falling into space. Then, as quick as a flash, I opened a flashing door and went through. I was falling through a black abyss. While I was falling, I heard screaming and crying. I kept hearing shouting from people.

After a bit, I started to see white stuff. "Snow!" I shouted. Then I hit the ground with a thud. When I got up, the sky was red but the ground was white. It was as hot as a desert but as cold as an iceberg. There were also meteors flying through the sky.

I saw a man in white clothes in front of me. He showed me around. It was like a tiny snowy village. Then I saw there was a massive, long wall. The man whispered, "Over there are the reds, they are the enemy, we don't talk about them." The man let me stay in his guest room, then I went to sleep.

I woke up in the middle of the night and thought, *shall I climb over the wall?* I climbed over the wall and saw lots of red houses.

Beau Bromley (9)
St Mary's Catholic Primary School, Broadway

Cosmic Scrub To Mars

I was in the rocket when the comms went offline. It was only ten seconds until launch. Our control screens were counting down: 3, 2, 1, lift-off! But nothing was happening. Suddenly, the comms came back on and said, "Launch scrubbed due to weather conditions."

After mission control gave us the go, I opened the metallic, safe-like hatch and marched down the crew access beam. Then I met the crew support team on the ground to give me and the rest of the crew a check. After I took my spacesuit off, I walked back to my quarters.

I opened the door to the crew quarters, but it led to a tunnel, not my quarters. After five minutes, the tunnel came to a fork. One side said, *Magical World* and the other side said, *Boring Apartments*. I chose 'magical world' as I felt a bit adventurous. A few minutes later, it came to another fork. One that said, *Venus* and one that said, *Mars*. I chose Mars this time, if I went to Venus I would burn to death.

After an hour or two, I came out of the tunnel at the other end. Everything was red, misty, and cold. For the first time, I could see Earth from another planet. Then there was a shadow in the distance. As it got closer and closer, I could make out that it was... an alien!

William Hobbs-Gray (9)
St Mary's Catholic Primary School, Broadway

Planet Breathable?

An extract

I woke up with one thought: food. Out of the corner of my eye, I saw Liam daydreaming out of the diamond-shaped window, staring at the galaxies ahead. I floated quietly past him. I started using the swimming moves the other dads taught me.

The metallic room was spinning out of control. I saw a floating chair so I grabbed it and tried to sit on it. Eventually, I got off the chair because it wasn't comfy. My tummy rumbled. I felt something cold and metal attached to the chair - a small metal key. It was purple with teal swirls and yellow lightning bolts.

I grabbed the key. Then something caught my eye, it was bright purple with teal swirls and yellow lighting bolts. I swam over to it. It was a door! I tried to pull it open but it was locked. I looked above, the door was engraved with Chinese letters. Then I recalled the key. The door opened. I heard a weird sucking noise, then I got sucked in.

When I woke up I was on a planet with oxygen. It wasn't like Earth, its atmosphere was swirly colours. Then I saw different shapes. I gave them names: Bob, Hob, Lob, Pob, and Dave. They had blood dripping all over them. They put a net on me and the next thing I knew, I was hovering above boiling hot water.

Emma Terefenko (9)
St Mary's Catholic Primary School, Broadway

The Magic Door

There were five of us on board, the others were asleep. We were drifting in space, out of control forever, can you believe it? Probably not. Their choice was a nap! I went to check on them, they were still asleep. I couldn't believe it, still fast asleep.

I went to the control room. Everything was flashing. All the buttons there were flashing red, green, yellow, and blue. There was one that stood out to me, it said, 'Fault'. I went to the tools. I unscrewed everything. Something fell. I went to pick it up.

I saw a hatch. I opened it and crawled through. It was a simulation all along! I went to wake them up. "Guys! Wake up!" I screamed. They were angry that I had woken them. I told them, "Come with me!" So they did. I said, "Come through here." They did it, we went through. It was a simulation. I saw a light, but there is no light in space. I crawled through and there were people out there. I asked, "Where am I?"

They said, "You were the first to figure it out." I was shocked that it wasn't real. I had lots of questions.

Harry Dempsey (9)
St Mary's Catholic Primary School, Broadway

Past The Creaky Door

There were five of us on board. The others were all asleep. Can you believe that, by the way? We were in a rocket, spinning hopelessly out of control and into forever, and their chosen course of action? A nap!

So as I, Liam Digby, was the only one awake, I was the responsible adult. I needed to find a way out of this spinning, crazy rocket. I decided to look around for a control manual.

I moved some boxes leaning on a blank white wall. A sign glimmered. It said, *Keep Out!* in big, bold letters. I felt anxious about what was inside, but I really needed to find the control manual, so I crept toward it and twisted the door handle.

All of a sudden, a big rush of wind hit me and pushed me back. I felt like I'd been through a big storm. I decided to try again. I ran at the door and pushed... I fell, but I didn't fall, I floated. I looked up and saw my parents, so I went toward them. Then they disappeared into thin air. I felt horror grip onto me.

Maddie Emms (10)
St Mary's Catholic Primary School, Broadway

Liam's Magic Door

Could you believe, me, a twelve-year-old, on a rocket going into space? Everyone's choice of action when we were doomed? A nap. So I started to look for a manual. I got off-track and looked around, how many times does a twelve-year-old get to be in a billion-dollar rocket?

I started opening everything, including hatches. Then I saw a glowing hatch. Above it said, *No Entry!* I opened it anyway. When I opened the red, metallic hatch, I thought, *what if this sends us into space?* I was too late.

When it opened, I saw red eyes that pulled me out of the rocket. It looked black. Black like a room with no lights on. Someone pulled me into another world. Next, I could smell raw beef and rotting sandwiches filled with sand. After that, aliens were trying to meet other aliens for jobs.

The job was getting humans to learn about them and study them. It was a secret plan since some people didn't like them.

Harry Tarte (9)
St Mary's Catholic Primary School, Broadway

Through The Hatch

Can you believe that, by the way? We were spinning, hopelessly out of control, and their chosen course of action was a nap! I decided to explore the rocket, opening every door, looking for a manual. I had no luck until I saw a hatch. It was metallic, it looked like a manual-holding hatch. I decided to fly over there. It easily swung open and I got teleported under the sea. It was dark blue. I couldn't breathe. I was astonished. I went from a rocket to the sea! I swam up to look around. All I could see was land until, at last, I could see a farm.

I went to ask him where I was. He exclaimed I was in Ireland. I couldn't believe it. I went from space to Ireland. I travelled, looking for more people. Eventually, I saw a village in the distance. I came to a house and saw an alien family. I was on a different planet! I had to get out of there.

Taylor Miller (9)
St Mary's Catholic Primary School, Broadway

The Magic Door

I just got out of bed and I was going to grab some crisps and watch TV. As I was watching TV, a strange bang came from upstairs but I ignored it. Another bang came from upstairs, so I went up and I saw a door! A strange door with lights and Christmas ornaments, so I thought it was jolly. I opened the door and a powerful suction sucked me in.

I could hear Christmas bells and Christmas music. I could feel snow and I could see Santa walking up to me, saying I was 'the one'. He said, "Lilly, you need to help, the Grinch is stealing Christmas!" He put me in the sleigh and off we went.

Now I was in the sky, I could see Christmas lights on every house and... wait a minute! I saw the Grinch, he was stealing Christmas. Now we were chasing the Grinch, he was going fast but... no, we lost him. Wait, no! He was chasing me now!

"Oh! I have got him! Santa! I've got him."

"Okay, I'm coming. Now you're going to prison. Well done, Lilly, you saved the day."

Lilly Arens (10)

St Mary's Catholic Primary School, Evesham

The Magic Door

I was playing with my friend. She went to the bathroom. She didn't come out, so I went to check on her but she wasn't there. I'd lost my best friend. I ran out of the bathroom and saw a purple door. I found myself turning the handle of the door. It opened. There was a shining swirl, so I walked through the door. It sucked me in. There was a sign that said, *Welcome To The Magic Door*. I thought it was a dream.

I closed my eyes, then I opened them. It was not a dream. It was like I was in another neighbourhood. People were staring at me like they were scared. I asked them to help me find my way back home. They said there was a wishing rock.

I asked them, "How does that work?"

They said, "You just have to make a wish."

"Where is it?"

"We don't know, nobody found it yet."

Hmm. I had an idea: I was going to find the rock. "Can someone help me?"

"Okay, we have to be careful because it is dangerous."

Hours went past and we were still at the bottom of the mountain. I saw something. "Come on, let's see what that is." We went down there - it was a volcano! It exploded!

"*Aah!* I tried to tell you there was a volcano. Wait, a rock! The wishing rock!"

"I wish to go back home!" *Boom!* Ahh, I was at home.

Weronika Grosfeld (8)

St Mary's Catholic Primary School, Evesham

The Magic Door

An extract

I was sitting on my bed, then my mum called me for dinner. When I opened my door, I saw a big house. I didn't know what it was, so I didn't want to go in. I closed the door. I opened the door again a few minutes later and went in.

Suddenly, I saw a big island and there were big houses connected to each other. I could see palm trees, people, and a massive ocean. I could hear people laughing, chatting, and splashing into the ocean. I could feel soft sand while I was walking. I could taste the water from the ocean.

Suddenly, I could smell a barbecue, it smelled delicious. When I walked to the back of the houses, there were kids and adults going down this yellow slide. All of a sudden, someone came up to me and said, "Why don't you come for some food? You must be very hungry and thirsty."

"Thank you, I'm very hungry and thirsty," I said happily.

I went into the house, it was so beautiful. They told me I could explore. I was shocked because I saw an indoor pool. They said that I could go in it, so they gave me a swimming suit and I put it on and went in.

A few hours later I got out of the pool. I said, "I think I need to go now because my mum is looking for me."
"Okay, but come back someday," said the person happily.

Samanta Witalec (9)
St Mary's Catholic Primary School, Evesham

The Magic Door

An extract

I was in my bedroom watching Haikyuu! As I opened the door, I walked in. Suddenly, out of nowhere, I spawned in another dimension! I realised I was at Haikyuu High School.

I heard noises from inside the building. I went inside and explored. I still couldn't see anyone. I noticed it was coming from the gym, so I peeked through the window. People were playing volleyball. As I was watching them play, someone behind me pushed me into the gym. Everyone was staring at me!

It was very embarrassing until Shoyo, my favourite character, helped me get up. Shoyo invited me into the game and he practised with me. As we started playing, I had the ball in my hands. I was sweaty and nervous. Shoyo told me to throw it in the air. I threw the ball and smacked it as hard as I could with my palm. It went flying in the air! It even went past Tobia, he is so tall!

Everyone was in shock. I realised this was really fun, even though I didn't know how to play. Sadly, we had a problem - we were only one point behind. Shoyo was very frustrated, so was I.

As the other team had the ball, our team had a plan. As they threw the ball, our eyes popped. I jumped as high as I could, and I did it! I threw the ball over the net and none of them caught it. The ball just hit the ground.

Oliwia Kustra (9)

St Mary's Catholic Primary School, Evesham

The Magic Door

One day, when I got out of my bed, I saw this mysterious glowing door. I was tempted to go through it. I went through the door and I landed in this mysterious place. I went to go and ask this strange-looking person where I was. He said Pompeii. I shrieked because my mum had mentioned Pompeii before as a really dangerous place. I ran away.

Later, I heard a roaring sound. I screamed. I followed the boiling lava. Crowds were running everywhere, I almost fell over. I kept on following the lava trail. Suddenly, I heard another roar. I tumbled over. I got back up. I didn't know if I should keep going or not. There were two lava trails going in opposite directions. I didn't know which way to go.

I went right. I couldn't hear any more roars. The trail stopped. I screamed. I'd gone the wrong way. I went back. I asked myself, "What is this mysterious thing?" I went left. I followed the trail until I saw what was causing this - a volcano!

I ran back through the houses, past the man, until I reached the magic door again. I went back in and landed back in my bedroom. I thought, *phew! That's over!* I went downstairs and had breakfast.

Sophia Dare (8)
St Mary's Catholic Primary School, Evesham

Back To Padstow Again

It is a grey, foggy November morning when I step through the door. I step into a whole different world: Padstow Harbour. I can feel my stomach bubble with excitement as I see the boats bobbing blissfully on the water.

I hear the gulls screech and cry, flapping madly around. I can smell the crispy, battered, lard-coated fish and deep-fried, golden-brown, chunky chips when the smell drifts out of the open window of the minuscule chip shop.

I wait in the queue of people, deciding what to have. When I order, I get a large fish and chips with orange juice and a whippy ice cream cone. While I sit and wait, I hear people crying their wares along the crooked, uneven, cobbled streets. I breathe in the fresh salty air.

When my food comes, I eat heartily. After I finish, I pay at the till and leave the chip shop. Next, I decide to go crab fishing, so I buy a bucket, net, and bait. I sit, my net hovering down into the freezing, clear harbour water.

Suddenly, I feel a tugging on my net. I slowly pull it up, revealing a minuscule scarlet crab. I examine it, then I lower it back into the water. It's time for me to go.

Jessica Whiting (10)

St Mary's Catholic Primary School, Evesham

The Magic Door

I was playing Minecraft when this portal that looked like a door appeared. I got my Netherite gear that was fully enchanted and went in.

I saw a dragon and Endermen - they are tall men with pitch-black skin with purple eyes. I could taste chorus fruit and I could hear the Enderdragon, his breath smelt like mouldy potatoes. I felt hard rock on my feet, then I noticed that I was in the end! The Enderdragon attacked me, then I turned and I was face-to-face with an Enderman. If you are face-to-face with an Enderman, it will attack. Then all of the Endermen would attack me. I fell off the edge.

I used an Ender pearl to get back on the End island, then killed the Endermen. I had to break the End crystals so the Enderdragon couldn't revive his health. Then I shot him out of the sky, then smacked him with my sword. He died.

I took his egg because it was one of a kind, then I took all of its XP because it had 65 XP levels, so I could enchant more stuff. Then the portal opened and a gateway opened.

But that was for another day, so I hopped into the portal and came out beside my bed and went to sleep.

Dexter Wright (9)

St Mary's Catholic Primary School, Evesham

The Magic Door

I don't know how it happened. I opened the Owl Class door and I found myself in a place where peace was forgotten. Dragons were flying around and fighting the volcanic magma. I was so confused, but there was no time to waste! I ran faster and faster until I was on a ship. I thought, *how is this possible? Maybe I travelled through a magic door.*

On the ship, I couldn't breathe. The ashes were spreading all around the island. I asked the ship's captain where we were. He said, "We are in Italy, Pompeii." I was shocked. I had a really long way home. I wasn't able to pay for the way home because I was only a child.

The Captain was that kind to take people to Italy and, especially for me, he went seven hours to England and called my mum to pick me up. When my mum picked me up, I told her all about my adventure. I told her the magic door looked like a door from Owl Class at school.

I said the weirdest part was when I was leaving Pompeii, the year was 79 AD. But when I got home, the year was 2022. Had I time travelled? That was the biggest question.

Jakub Kupejtys (9)

St Mary's Catholic Primary School, Evesham

The Adventures In Pompeii

Dear reader, if you are reading this, my adventures in Pompeii have concluded. My name is Ruairidh Marlborough and I am escaping Pompeii in a merchant ship. Wondering where I am from? Let's rewind to the beginning...

Dear Diary,

Today was the weirdest day ever. I got out of bed and opened my door and what did I see? A magnificent city! I walked through the doorway, thinking I was hallucinating. Big mistake! I ended up in a theatre where a play was being rehearsed. I saw my friend Dominik and I shouted hello. Then I left.

Dear Diary,

I now have some togas. Suddenly, the Earth began to shake and the sky began to darken. I ran outside to see what was going on and then Mt Vesuvius blew its top! It sounded like a kettle that had exploded. It started as a hiss, then a buzz, then *boom!* A glistening, silver ash cloud was raining down.

I decided I needed to move. In a matter of seconds, I was in the theatre but the door had gone, so I ran to a merchant ship. I have just seen Dominik on the deck. Goodbye and good luck.

Ruairidh Marlborough (8)
St Mary's Catholic Primary School, Evesham

The Magic Door

I was just sitting in my garden when, suddenly, a strange door popped out of the sky with mysterious blue mist and thorny vines coming out of it. When it finally hit the ground, I opened it and went inside.

To my surprise, I got teleported to a jungle of some sort. I could see toucans drifting in the air, frogs leaping around. Then I hit the ground with a toucan slamming into me. The toucan was soaking and shivering, and that was when I started to hear growling.

I looked down to see a baby jaguar by my feet, and the mother arrived. I slowly walked backwards, then I hit my head on a tree which woke the baby jaguar. So then the mum started to chase me through the dark damp forest.

The toucan from earlier snuck into my bag, then it flew into a small gap that the jaguar couldn't fit in, so the jaguar then went back to where it lived.

Now I retraced my steps back to the magical door and got to my home with my new friend toucan, just in time for my food. What an adventure!

Jack Kingsbury (9)

St Mary's Catholic Primary School, Evesham

The Magic Door

This morning, I was peacefully in my comfy, warm bed, watching football highlights. Then I went downstairs for some hot buttery toast. It was very tasty. I was still very tired, so I went back to my room. I opened my door and...

I was in a humongous football stadium! But there was a terrible thing about it: the crowd were very, very loud. For a second, I thought I would go deaf. But then, something horrifying happened. Also, it smelt horrific.

The horrifying thing was that everybody got into a huge argument! The referee got involved, so I thought I should get involved to try and stop it.

"Finally!" said the crowd. Finally, the argument had happily been solved. Luckily, the referee solved it by giving out a lot of red cards.

Finally, after a long time, I thought it was time to go back through the door. After a long travel back to the door, I finally reached it. I stepped back through the door and, yes, I was finally back in my beautiful bedroom.

Jacob Hughes (8)
St Mary's Catholic Primary School, Evesham

The Magic Door

One day, I found a little magic door and I walked through it. It made a loud noise when it opened and it took me to an exciting new land: Pompeii. Pompeii looked dangerous, I thought.

I heard people screaming loudly and the massive volcano shooting out grey ash clouds, it was hot and windy. I saw people taking their belongings and getting to safety. Two girls were crying because they were lost. I wanted to help but I was too nervous.

I shouted to them. They told me their names were Mary and Lily. We saw a boat and jumped onto it and then we rowed onto the water. Life on the boat was hard. We went to different places.

First, we went to a cold place. "It's too cold," said Mary.

Then we went to a hot place. "It's too hot," said Lily.

Then we tried a small place where it was warm and safe. "It's wonderful," I shouted. We built our home there and became best friends. Maybe people wanted to live there.

Eva Fairburn-Shead (7)

St Mary's Catholic Primary School, Evesham

The Magic Door

I was sitting on my bed. I saw this strange door. I was freaked out. I wanted to go in it. I thought to myself, *should I go in or not?* I said, "I will go in." And I went in.

I was in a football stadium. I could see football goals. I also heard the crowd cheering. It was hot and warm. I could feel the wind trying to blow the ball everywhere. It went in the goal.

Then I saw people climbing over the stadium fence because the tickets for the football were £1000, so I went to the bathroom to get away and think of a plan to stop people climbing over. I thought to myself that I should stop it. I had an idea, I dressed up as a police officer and sorted it out.

When the problem was sorted, I tried to find the magic door. I kept searching. I found it in the locker. I got back home and my mum called me for dinner. My dinner was hot so I went to my bedroom. I saw the magic door disappear and my mum called me again.

William Kizas (9)

St Mary's Catholic Primary School, Evesham

The Adventures In A Forest

It was a rainy day as I stepped through the door that took me to the best place I could imagine: it was a green, breezy forest. The forest looked like it was endless. I could stay here for life if I wanted to. As I stepped in, I started to hear something in the bushes. I thought it was an animal, so I ignored it. I got deeper and deeper into the forest and it turned out the mysterious creature was following me. I wanted to see what it was, but I got goosebumps thinking about it, so I just stood there glaring into the bush, my mood swinging like crazy from curious, to nervous, and after that, terror.
I stood there until I gathered up the courage to see what it was. Two seconds later, I thought I was being a dramatic scaredy-cat! I was brave enough to look. I went closer and grabbed the bushes, hoping not to get bitten, and shook them a little. What I saw surprised me - it was a ginger baby fox.

Weronika Jaskulska
St Mary's Catholic Primary School, Evesham

Going To Disneyland With The Magic Door

It was an amazing morning. I was sitting in my house, doing nothing. I remembered that I had a magic door that a fairy gave me and I could use it one time. I decided to go to my favourite place: Disneyland! Then I rushed to my magic door and said, "I want to go to Disneyland."
I closed my eyes and jumped inside. I couldn't believe my eyes, it was my dream place. There were amazing rides like roller coasters. My mouth watered when I saw yummy sweetshops. Then I heard a wonderful Disney song. Not only that, there were beautiful princesses standing in a carriage and they had their princes.
When I saw them, my eyes went open and my mouth too. My hands were raised up to them. Then Rapunzel caught my hand and blew a kiss to me and I was like, "I am going to blackout!" After that, I saw the castle! I was over the moon. I saw Mickey Mouse and other characters

Riya Elsa Joby (10)
St Mary's Catholic Primary School, Evesham

The Magic Door

On a rainy, stormy day, I was playing Pac-Man, then my mum called me for dinner. I opened my bedroom door and then I went downstairs to something wonderful... I was thrilled to see that I was in Pac-Man!

Every step, I could see 10-foot walls and the two best things I saw were berries and pineapple. Then I kept on hearing creaking on the floor, which was very awkward because who would come to this mucky, disgusting hallway?

I had goosebumps and was shivering. I hated being cold, it was terrible. I was walking, then I heard a noise coming from the end of the hallway. It was Pac-Man and the ghosts!

I ran for my life. I didn't want to get eaten by Pac-Man. Then I saw a corner, I turned and saw the magic door. I finally got home. My mum was so confused that I didn't come down for my tuna pasta bake. I was so sad, I missed my favourite dinner.

Luca Kear-Bertie (9)

St Mary's Catholic Primary School, Evesham

The Dream Theater Concert

It was a cold, dark evening. The atmosphere thrilled in anticipation of the concert. I heard the loud screams as Dream Theater walked on stage. I saw millions of people waiting for the start of the concert.

As time passed, I smelt hot dogs and pizzas the stalls were selling. As I heard somebody say they would start soon, they started to tune their guitars and Mike Portnoy sat at his drum set. Five minutes later, they started.

I couldn't believe my eyes. I was at a Dream Theater concert. I was a bit stupid getting tickets at the front row, because I found myself in the middle of a mosh pit. I really didn't care because they were playing my favourite song: Breaking All Illusions. I thought I was the happiest kid alive. Three hours later, the concert finished and I got a t-shirt signed by John Petrucci, Mike Portnoy and James Labre.

Joshua Hosken (10)
St Mary's Catholic Primary School, Evesham

The Magic Door

I spawned by walking in my friend's door. And my friends, Jack and Noah, were there for some reason. I felt clueless and scared. I saw a statue in the middle, a staircase next to it. Then I smelt smoke.

Noah whispered, "I failed the hack."

I said, "What hack?" then I heard a heartbeat in the distance.

Then I saw a person with a hammer. She hit Noah and put him in a tube. He was starting to freeze. We freed him and ran out of there. After we tried hacking, the magic door was then able to open. We could leave, at last.

Finally, we dodged and weaved the beast's attacks. The beast was chasing us. We opened the door, but Jack - we realised he was hit on the way without us noticing. We freed him. I got hit but I got saved. We just got out alive. The beast looked familiar... It was my older cousin, Orlagh.

Logan Hart (9)

St Mary's Catholic Primary School, Evesham

The Magic Door

When I woke up, I was getting dressed and when I tried to get out of my room, the door opened and there was a beam of light. A sign said, *Warning! No Entrance Or There Is A Consequence Of Death*. I went in the door and I was at Mt Vesuvius. Me and Lewis Hamilton were in the volcano. We were so hot that we were overheating. We found another sign, it said, *I Told You There Will Be Consequences*.

It was so hot. We heard a rumble. Hamilton got me and him fireproof suits, so when it erupted we wouldn't burn. The volcano erupted. We were okay because we had fireproof suits.

We landed in the ocean. We swam back to the shore. We arrived at Pompeii, it was beautiful. I wanted to live there. We found another door, it said, *You Need To Go Home*. I woke up. It was a dream. I loved it.

Zach Thompson (8)
St Mary's Catholic Primary School, Evesham

The Magic Door

One day, I went to school as usual but there was a mysterious wall with a faint line on it. It perked up my imagination. I pushed the line, it quivered. It broke open with a huge light. It sucked me in. Wow, this was for real.

I found myself in a new world. It looked like a theatre. My friend, Ruairidh, shouted hello to me. It was strange. He wore a toga and I wore a PE kit. Ruairidh invited me to his house. I gazed around in amazement. This world was so different. When I arrived at Ruairidh's house, I asked him where we were. He said, "Pompeii. It has a volcano."

Boom! Crack! Fshoo! Agh! Vesuvius was erupting! Me and Ruairidh rapidly ran to the shore. I felt burning magma. We saved each other's lives dozens of times. We jumped into the water and found ourselves back at school.

Dominik Gyorgy (8)

St Mary's Catholic Primary School, Evesham

New York City

As I opened the door, I could hear the busy streets of New York City. I desperately ran through the door, eager to see all the giant towers and skyscrapers. As I walked around the top floor of Central Park Tower, I couldn't help but notice that it was an apartment. I could hear all the people talking to room service and people on their phones.

As I went down in the elevator, I saw lots of families playing in the park. I went out of Central Park Tower and immediately got a taxi and asked the driver to give me a tour of New York. We drove round the streets and houses, avoiding all the crazy drivers.

At lunchtime, we stopped at McDonald's and ordered a McChicken Sandwich. I could smell my food being prepared. I went back to Central Park Tower just in time for bed.

Frank Johnson (10)
St Mary's Catholic Primary School, Evesham

Sugar Land

I wasn't supposed to, but I did it. I found myself turning the knob of the new, shiny classroom door. Then I went outside for a breather, but outside looked different...

The school was now gingerbread, the trees were candy canes, and a hill that I had never seen before was standing in the distance. I looked down, the pebbles were chocolate! I looked up, the clouds were cotton candy!

I rushed inside. I told everyone but they said, "Oh please, do you think we will believe such a story?" I mumbled and grumbled, then I stopped making noises but the grumbling didn't stop.

I looked at Mt Sugarpuff and syrup was pouring out of the top! It got closer to me. A nearby candy cane tree was melting in the syrup. Then it melted me and I died.

Harry Simpson (8)

St Mary's Catholic Primary School, Evesham

The Magic Door

I wasn't supposed to, but I did it! I found myself turning the handle of the magic door. It sucked me in! I suddenly found myself in a strange new world. I couldn't believe it, I was in Pompeii!

I looked around and I could see people walking in and out of doors everywhere. It was busy. I couldn't believe my eyes, it was horrendous - the pizza restaurant was full.

Suddenly, I saw dark clouds, as dark as a really dark dog. I saw the volcano erupting. Everyone was running in fear. This was it, the moment I was waiting for, the erupting volcano, it was the end of me!

Or was it? I was terrified. I jumped in a random boat. I fell asleep. When I woke up, I saw Pompeii, it was getting smaller and smaller. I saw a man, the man that saved me.

Ella-Rose Bools (7)

St Mary's Catholic Primary School, Evesham

Through The Magic Door To Paris

It was a cold, windy evening as I stepped into the magic door and saw the best place in the world: Paris. The capital city of France. Paris looked glamorous and beautiful, I felt like the luckiest person in the world.

I felt like I was in a dream. I went to the one place I had always wanted to go if I ever visited Paris, the Eiffel Tower. The Eiffel Tower looked stunning and magical. It was the best time of my life. Then I went to a restaurant and the food there was mouth-watering and scrumptious. It was the best food I had ever tasted.

The street was full of people talking and shouting, even rock songs playing. I felt the warm evening air swirl around me and it felt amazing. I was on cloud nine. I even felt butterflies fluttering in my stomach.

Rebecca Adenuga (10)

St Mary's Catholic Primary School, Evesham

The Magic Door

I was in my room and I was playing Minecraft. My controller ran out of battery, so I went downstairs to get my dad's charger. He was in the living room. He started floating. I looked down and... now I was in Minecraft!

I went down and found a pond, so I went swimming. I went exploring and found a dog. I named it Christopher. I built an oak plank house and slept very well. I went mining but when I came back with my five diamonds, my door was open and Christopher was gone!

I looked for days but he was nowhere to be found, so I cried. I carried on looking for my dog and then, in the corner of my eye, I saw him. He betrayed me! He ran to me in an evil way, so I found the door and ran into it and got home safely. And I brought my diamonds.

Henry Resende (9)

St Mary's Catholic Primary School, Evesham

Through The Magic Door To Wembley Football Stadium

It was a chilly morning in November as I stepped through the magic door and I saw the most exciting place in the world: Wembley Football Stadium! The best place to go and enjoy yourself. The stadium stood in front of me and all I could hear was shouting from cheering fans.

The stadium was enormous and beautiful. I felt joyful and energetic, like I was about to play the match. The seats were full of cheering fans making ear-splitting noise and singing in anticipation for the teams, who were about to start playing.

As I sat down, I could smell food, juices, and sweets. When the players started coming out onto the pitch, they stood in a straight line because they wanted to sing the national anthem. After a moment, they started playing.

Nothando Ganse (10)

St Mary's Catholic Primary School, Evesham

The Great Football Stadium

It was an icy evening as I walked through the door that took me to the place I had always dreamed of going, the best place in the whole entire universe: a football stadium!

The stadium was in front of me like Mount Everest reaching to the sky. I could see the curvy roof reaching into each other. The seats were all full of excited people ready to start cheering and chanting.

After a while, the game started, everyone was excited and nervous at the same time, wondering how the game would go.

The tension was rising as the ball was heading towards the opposition's net, then all of a sudden the ball went in, smashing the back of it.

Everyone raised the roof!

Orlagh Turner (10)

St Mary's Catholic Primary School, Evesham

All On A Sunny Day

I opened the door. I stepped inside. The crystal-clear waves lapped softly onto the smooth sand. The tatty dock stretched across the glistening water to reach the strange cabin.

A mysterious crab appeared out of the microscopic sand and waddled slowly toward the calming sea. The clouds, like fluffy cotton candy, floated in the luminous sky as the birds glided through the air. As I stood on the soothing sand, the gentle breeze travelled through my hair. The taste of salt in the swift air reached my tastebuds, it was as salty as anchovies. The palm trees, as tall as mountains, waved their hands in the cooling breeze of the air as they stood firmly on the rocky ground.

David Rusnak (11)
St Mary's Catholic Primary School, Evesham

The Magic Door

I was outside with my friend. We saw a door that said: *Don't Enter*, but we went in. We were in a different world. It was so peaceful, but then the floor started to shake. It was an earthquake!
I could see Pompeii. There was ashy air, I couldn't breathe. Then lava came out. The birds were flying all around. I followed everyone but I realised I was in school shoes. I took a rest, then the earthquake ended and it was peaceful again.
"It finally stopped!" I was so happy, but I couldn't find the door. We found the door but it was locked. We were scared but someone gave us a drink. We survived. Everyone was super happy.

Anastazia Kalinska (7)

St Mary's Catholic Primary School, Evesham

Qatar Football Stadium

It's an ice-cold evening as I walk through the door.
Then I see the Qatar football stadium, the most
exciting place on Earth. The seats are full of people
chanting and waving flags.

I can smell the wonderful smell of buttery popcorn,
fish and chips, and nacho cheese. I can feel my
heart starting to race with excitement and joy. I
can hear people arguing and debating about
which team will win.

While people are cheering, the football stars show
up. Then some people stop and pull out their
cameras. You can only see a bunch of cameras
flashing in your eyes while the stars sing their
national anthem.

Michal Skowronski (10)

St Mary's Catholic Primary School, Evesham

The Magic Door

I wasn't supposed to do this, but I wanted to. I found a mysterious door, then I turned the door handle. My dad had told me not to open the door. My dog, called Ruby, barged into me, then we ended up falling in.

I found out that we were in Pompeii. I found a cottage for sale. I gave the person money. I made the house look cosy and soft. I made jumpers for me and Ruby. I looked for my dog's leash and saw a little kitten in the sun. I let it in and gave it food and water.

I called the kitten Avery. I made her a little jumper with a Christmas tree on it. I made Avery a bed with a pillow.

Joanna Watalska (8)

St Mary's Catholic Primary School, Evesham

Turning Into A Mushroom

I was bored in my room. I was going to watch TV but the downstairs TV was bigger. I ran through the door. I went to a magic land.

In a second, I turned into a super cute mushroom with arms and legs. The magic land had lovely flowers and the sunrise was beautiful.

I was minding my own business and a squirrel tried to get me. I just escaped the squirrel. To my surprise, I saw lots of mushrooms. I went with them and we had dinner. It was wet leaves, I ate fifty of them.

I said I needed to go, then the mushrooms made a tower. I went through the door. I took the mushrooms and they loved it.

Kipras Price (8)
St Mary's Catholic Primary School, Evesham

The Boy Who Went Through A Door

Once upon a time, I was in my room and a magic door appeared by my bed. I ran as quick as a flash. I went through the magic door and I was at the North Pole.

An elf told me that the sleigh was broken and it was nearly morning. The elf garage was far away. But one elf was on a polar bear. The elf got off the polar bear and ran up the steep mountain.

At last, the elf saw the sleigh. The elf said to pull up the sleigh and the elf ran to the garage and took the tools to mend the sleigh. Then the magic door opened and I walked back through the door.

Felix Hudson (5)
St Mary's Catholic Primary School, Evesham

The World Cup Final

It's a cold November evening as I step through the magic door and see one of the best places in the world: Qatar football stadium, the home of the 2022 World Cup.

The stadium is as tall as a mountain, I can see people wearing their team shirts as I enter the stadium. I can smell mouthwatering food like burgers, hot dogs, and chips covered in delicious red ketchup.

Silence covers the whole stadium as we wait for the teams to enter the pitch. Brazil enter first, then Argentina.

Albert Duta (10)

St Mary's Catholic Primary School, Evesham

The Huge Mansion

It was an icy morning as I stepped through the magic door that took me to the place I never wanted to leave: a huge mansion. As I moved my head around, I saw a grand piano that was as big as my whole bedroom.

I saw some luxurious stairs that led to the second floor. They were covered with real gold too. I started strolling and happily climbed them. I couldn't believe it, there were probably a million scented candles that smelt like the best vanilla you could imagine.

Olivia Kilian (10)

St Mary's Catholic Primary School, Evesham

Monkeys

Once upon a time, a magic door appeared in my room. As quick as a flash, I ran to the door. When I opened it, I was surprised I was in the jungle.
When I went through the jungle, I met monkeys who were holding bananas. A bird came down and tried to eat the bananas. The monkeys were trying to chase away the bird.
I said, "I've got seeds." The bird flew down to me and ate the seeds. The monkeys were happy. Next, the magic door came back.

Jack Ciesar (6)
St Mary's Catholic Primary School, Evesham

The Magic Door

I was at school when I went to my locker. I opened it and there was a long portal. It sucked me in as fast as a cheetah. I dropped my books when I was sucked in.

It was a long journey to Pompeii. I was speechless. I was surprised. I was lost, so I walked down the hill and I got closer to the town. Suddenly, someone saw me and said I was an intruder. They chased me.

The sun was as hot as lava. Then, *bang!* Everyone trembled.

Olivia Nind (8)

St Mary's Catholic Primary School, Evesham

The Magic Door

I was at school. I wanted to go to the toilet. I opened the door. I was thinking, *how did I get here?* I was on a roller coaster.

When the roller coaster was going, I was screaming. As it was going, there was a hot, horrible smell and a toxic taste. But the roller coaster did not stop.

I saw a lever to stop the roller coaster. I pulled the lever. I closed my eyes, then I opened my eyes. I was at my school desk.

Leon Philip (8)

St Mary's Catholic Primary School, Evesham

Blue Sea Adventure

Once upon a time, I saw a magic door appear. I went through it and I was in the blue sea. Next, I swam with the starfish, dolphins, and rainbow fish. Suddenly, a big blue shark came and wanted to eat all the fish. Then I got a long stick and scared him away. The fish were happy.
Finally, I found the magic door and opened it. I was home again.

Blanka Indyk (5)
St Mary's Catholic Primary School, Evesham

The Lonely Octopus

Once upon a time, I was in my room and I saw a magic door, so I went through the magic door. Suddenly, I fell onto a pirate ship. A giant octopus grabbed the pirate ship and it was sinking! After a while, it sunk to the bottom of the sea. But we figured out the octopus just wanted a friend. Then I saw a sparkling gift.

Rohan Wright (5)
St Mary's Catholic Primary School, Evesham

The Bad Pixie

One day, I went to my garden to water my flowers and I saw something strange in the distance. It was a door that went to a magical forest. A naughty pixie was destroying the magic crystal that belonged to the good fairies. I shot smoke at her and made her good. Finally, I went home.

Erin Fitzpatrick (5)
St Mary's Catholic Primary School, Evesham

Shark Fish

One day I saw a magic door appear. I opened it and I was in the blue sea. Next, a big shark came and wanted to eat the little fish. I found a very long stick and threw it at him. The shark swam away. Finally, the magic door opened and I was home.

Cristian La Barbera (5)

St Mary's Catholic Primary School, Evesham

Christmas Land

One day, a magic door appeared. I went in through the door and was at the North Pole. Then I saw the Grinch trying to take down the Christmas lights. I pressed the alarm and he ran away. Finally, I went through the magic door and was home.

Ava Withers (5)
St Mary's Catholic Primary School, Evesham

When I Went To Fairy Land

Once upon a time, a door appeared in my room. I took two steps and I was in Fairy Land. Next, one fairy told me about an evil witch. After that, I saw a snowmobile and the fairy was happy. Finally, I found the magic door. Then I was home.

Esther Olabamiji (6)
St Mary's Catholic Primary School, Evesham

The Lost Dragon

Once upon a time, there was a magic door. Then I saw a forest and a dragon was stuck. I threw a stick and the dragon caught it like a dog. The dragon was free. Finally, I went home through the magical door.

Anthoina Podsada (5)
St Mary's Catholic Primary School, Evesham

The Magic Door

Once upon a time, a magic door appeared in my room. I went to the North Pole and saw an elf. The Grinch had taken the Christmas tree lights. The elf went to get the Christmas tree lights. Then I went home.

Foster Marlborough (5)
St Mary's Catholic Primary School, Evesham

The Fish Friends

Once upon a time, I saw a magic door. Then when I got in, I was under the sea. Then a fish told me that a shark ate his friend. Then he got his friend back. Suddenly, the magic door came back.

Theo Lancaster (5)

St Mary's Catholic Primary School, Evesham

The Magic Door

A magic door was in my bedroom. I opened the door. There was fire, it was very hot. There were ash clouds around me. A volcano had erupted. I ran to the sea.

Udyat Udyat (7)
St Mary's Catholic Primary School, Evesham

The Magic Door

Once upon a time, I saw the rainbow fish. Then I walked to the fish. And finally, the fish became my friend.

Aeiden Reigon (5)

St Mary's Catholic Primary School, Evesham

The Magic Door

Once upon a time, there was a girl called Mia. She lived in a beautiful house. A small, brick house. She was playing with her toys. She found a door that she had never seen, but she didn't open it.
She found the doorbell and she pressed the button. It went *ding-ding!* But no one answered. Then she turned the key. She went through the door. She came to a land called Fairy Land. She saw a fairy!
She saw another fairy. The fairy that she saw before was an evil fairy. She was tricking Mia. The other fairy was a good fairy. Mia went with the evil fairy! She didn't know that the fairy was evil.
"Should I go by myself?" she said to herself.
The fairy heard her and said, "No, I know where to go, you don't."
"Okay, okay," said Mia.
"I need to go to my friend's house," said the evil fairy.

She was hiding from Mia but she noticed her. The good fairy attacked and she won the battle. She gave Mia some fairy dust she whispered to her, "Come again, bring the fairy dust and sprinkle it over your head and you will have fairy wings and you will fly!"
So Mia went back through the door and came back to her house.

Cara (7)
Trinity Oaks CE Primary School, Horley

The Magic Door

Once upon a time, there were two brothers, a little brother called James and a big brother called Mount. They were secret spies. They went to a secret base and they lived in a mansion.

One normal, ordinary day, they went on a horse to go to the park. They came home. The little brother James saw a magic door with a key in the lock.

James said, "Shall I open the door?"

Mount said, "Yes." They opened the door together. They went in through the door.

Suddenly, they were in a scary place full of devils. The brothers said, "Hello, what's your name?"

"My name is Bobby, I'm going to eat you up!"

The brothers ran for their lives back to the door! The big brother said, "I will open the door!" The door opened, *swish!* They were home safe.

"Let's go put the magic key in the safe." They opened the safe and locked it up. "Let's go and play football."

"Okay, you're goalie!"

Lincoln Pulham (7)

Trinity Oaks CE Primary School, Horley

The Magic Door

Once, there was a child called Jack. He lived in a lovely house. He asked his mum to go outside. He played happily. He played with his friends. They were playing with his frisbee. He threw the frisbee into the window.

They wanted Jack to get the frisbee. Jack opened the door. He went into the door and popped out. He saw a beautiful view in Dinosaur Land. He explored Dinosaur Land. Something was coming... then he saw a T-rex!

He ran for his life. The T-rex turned back. He finally stopped running. Then he looked up, he saw a van. He went inside the van, it was empty. He had his driving license on him. He drove until he met a dead end. Then he saw the T-rex again.

He ran through the forest and he hid behind a tree. He found some mud and put it on him so the T-rex couldn't smell him. The T-rex turned around. Then Jack went back to the door. He ran through the old, wooden door. He went back to his house. He went upstairs into his room.

Harrison Thompson-Gay (7)
Trinity Oaks CE Primary School, Horley

The Magic Door

She opened the colourful, shiny door. She grabbed the handle. She gasped, "I am in Ocean World! I am a mermaid!"

"Hello, my name is Megan. Here, I'll give you a shell."

"Wow, what is all this?"

"It's the Kingdom of the Ocean."

"Wow, I wanna race!"

"Okay, but I will win! Ready, steady, go!"

"I win."

"Yep, you win."

"Yay, thank you, see you tomorrow."

"Yeah, race tomorrow! I will win."

She went back through the colourful, shiny door. She went back home and played with her toys. She opened the secret door again. "Do you want to play games?"

"Yes, follow me," said Megan.

"Yay, my favourite game! What can we do now?"

"Race?"

"Yes, race!"

Thando Samira Muringai (6)

Trinity Oaks CE Primary School, Horley

The Magic Door

One fine, normal day, Lucy was watching a movie. Lucy was a sweet little girl. She lived with her dad and her sister, called Angela. Angela was going to get some popcorn, she told her sister to get the sweet popcorn.

Lucy went to the back garden. She saw a small, little door! It had a little shell, and she also saw a small, golden key. Lucy carefully opened the small, blue door. She saw so much water!

"Do you know what that means? It's an ocean!" Lucy said. "It's not just any ocean, it's a pink sea!" Lucy dived into the fresh, pink sea until she bumped into an evil jellyfish.

"Run!" said a mermaid.

They had food together. Lucy said, "I have to go."

Georgina Varghese (6)

Trinity Oaks CE Primary School, Horley

The Magic Door

Once upon a time, there was a small house and there was a pretty girl called Freya. She was a fun person. She found a small fairy shed. She was going to open the shed door, but she saw a massive spider. She was so scared, she freaked out so much. She shut the door. She opened the door again and the spider was gone. She went into the ocean world. Oh no! She saw an evil goldfish but a little mermaid and Freya fought it and they won. She loved this place. Then it was time to go.

Freya Wicks (6)
Trinity Oaks CE Primary School, Horley

The Magic Door

Once upon a time, there lived a boy called Robin. He was a good boy. He was very good at football. He saw a door with a gold, shiny, smooth door handle. It was cool.

He started to walk back home when a cat walked out. The name on the collar was Jack. He was in a weird place. There was an old wooden post. Then Robin saw the door again.

He walked to the old, creepy, wooden, scary door and opened it. Then he ran home and had some nice warm doughnuts.

Digby (7)
Trinity Oaks CE Primary School, Horley

The Magic Door

Once upon a time, there was a boy called Ron. Ron loved to play football in his garden. Ron was playing football in his garden, then he accidentally kicked the ball into the shed.

Ron went to get the ball. Ron saw some stairs, they were heading down. Ron saw something white. Ron saw some footballs. Ron saw some pitches.

He nearly saw everything. Ron couldn't believe it. It was nearly bedtime so he went back home.

Edward Meech (6)
Trinity Oaks CE Primary School, Horley

The Magic Door

Once upon a time, there was a little girl called Zoey who lived in a cottage. One sunny day, she was playing in her garden when she saw an old door. She twisted the door handle. She went inside. She fell down. She said, "Where am I?"
She saw a pot of gold by a rainbow but an evil leprechaun was guarding it. She went over there and hid in the bushes. She saw a fairy. She went at the leprechaun. She defeated him.

Rafael Sweeney (6)
Trinity Oaks CE Primary School, Horley

The Magic Door

Once upon a time, there was a pickle. His name was Mr Pickle. He worked at the pizza place. Then he ran out of tomatoes. He went to the shed to get some more and the door was creepy. But then the door opened and he went into Game Land! He found an evil coin.

Drew Bastin-Curd (7)

Trinity Oaks CE Primary School, Horley

The Magic Door

Once upon a time, they lived in a house. They went outside. Suddenly, they found a door. They opened the old, metal door. They went in through the door and saw an evil robot man! They had an intense battle and won. The evil robot had fought but the boy won.

Max O'Driscoll (7)

Trinity Oaks CE Primary School, Horley

Young Writers Information

We hope you have enjoyed reading this book – and that you will continue to in the coming years.

If you're the parent or family member of an enthusiastic poet or story writer, do visit our website **www.youngwriters.co.uk/subscribe** and sign up to receive news, competitions, writing challenges and tips, activities and much, much more! There's lots to keep budding writers motivated!

If you would like to order further copies of this book, or any of our other titles, then please give us a call or order via your online account.

Young Writers
Remus House
Coltsfoot Drive
Peterborough
PE2 9BF
(01733) 890066
info@youngwriters.co.uk

Join in the conversation!
Tips, news, giveaways and much more!

  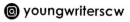

f YoungWritersUK   **🐦** YoungWritersCW   **📷** youngwriterscw